THE
Back Passage

THE
Back Passage

James Lear

Copyright © 2006 by James Lear.

All rights reserved. Except for brief passages quoted in newspaper, magazine, radio, television, or online reviews, no part of this book may be reproduced in any form or by any means, electronic or mechanical, including photocopying, recording, or information storage or retrieval system, without permission in writing from the publisher.

Published in the United States by Cleis Press Inc.,
P.O. Box 14697, San Francisco, California 94114.

Printed in the United States.
Cover design: Scott Idleman
Cover photograph: © 2006 by Louis LaSalle, www.louislasalle.com
Text design: Frank Wiedemann
Cleis logo art: Juana Alicia

First Edition.
10 9 8 7 6 5

Library of Congress Cataloging-in-Publication Data

Lear, James, 1960-
The back passage / by James Lear.—1st ed.
   p. cm.
ISBN 1-57344-243-7 (pbk. : alk. paper)
1. Murder—Investigation—England—Fiction. 2. Upper class—England—Fiction. 3. Americans—England—Fiction. 4. Gay men—Fiction. I. Title.
 PR6069.M543B33 2006
 823'.92—dc22
                                            2006006030

I

IT WAS THE HOTTEST DAY OF THE SUMMER OF 1925, with temperatures in the high 80s—not the ideal conditions for being indoors, in formal attire, squeezed into small, cramped spaces with other overheated, overdressed bodies. But, this being a country house weekend, and organized games being the order of the day, we had little choice, my fellow guests and I, but to play along with the whims of our hosts. And the whim of Sir James Eagle and his wife, Lady Caroline, was that we should play a game called Sardines.

Where I come from, sardines are something eaten by those who can't afford cod. But I was far from home in 1925. The north coast of Norfolk, England, where I was sweltering on that August afternoon, is a mighty long way from Boston, Massachusetts, and the large townhouse where I was born and whence I set out, a year ago to pursue postgraduate studies at Cambridge University.

Forgive the tedious details; what you really want to know is that I was squeezed into a cupboard under the stairs, usually used for storing croquet mallets and raincoats, with my best friend from Cambridge, Harry "Boy" Morgan—athlete, rowing blue, indifferent scholar, sweetheart of the daughter of the house—whose long, stiff cock was about to make its first-ever entrance into another man's mouth, namely, mine. I had been pursuing "Boy" Morgan, so named for his absurdly fresh, outdoorsy looks, his rangy limbs, his high spirits, and tendency, despite dark coloring, to blush easily, ever since I first caught sight of him carrying an upended rowboat from the waters of the Isis. His arms, raised above his head, were all long curves and elegant lines; his armpits, sweaty from his waterborne efforts, were matted with damp hair. The vest and shorts that he wore for training were likewise damp, and he smelled of strenuous athletic endeavor. If that weren't enough, he had smiled at me—a goofy, trusting smile of unquestioning welcome, which the new Yank in town had not always been given by the inward-looking burghers of Cambridge, who loved our new-world money but not our new-world manners.

I swore to myself that day by the river that I would have Boy Morgan by hook or by crook, and no amount of innocence, incomprehension, or downright stupidity on his part was going to stand in my way. Nor was the fact that he was recently engaged to the lovely and popular Miss Belinda Eagle, the sister of a teammate. I launched a campaign of teas in my rooms, of little lunches in Cambridge pubs washed down with pints of warm, flat Cambridge beer, of jolly afternoons punting down the Cam, of long, studious evenings in my rooms when I would guide him through the studies, easy for me, that defeated him.

Finally, during the long vacation, he'd taken pity on a lonely foreigner and secured me an invitation to beautiful Drekeham Hall, the Eagle family seat a stone's throw from the crumbly cliffs of the north Norfolk coast, for my first experience of the English upper classes in full cry. And now, in the darkness of a musty cupboard off the main stairwell, my campaign was about to be crowned with success. As I closed in on the prize, the musky smell of overheated athlete overpowered the ambient odor of Wellington boots and linseed oil. I could only imagine the burning blush on Morgan's cheeks, the parted lips, the dark hair tumbling from its brilliantined neatness. I could only imagine the thick vein swelling on his pale, high forehead, just as it did when he exerted himself at the oars. And I could only imagine his cock, which I had seen so many times in changing rooms and during our skinny-dipping jaunts in the river (how many of *those* had I organized!), now almost entirely hard, about to be swallowed and tasted, every long, lean inch of it.

And how, you may ask, had I engineered this situation? I had hardly done a thing; the manners and mores of the time did my work for me. We were sharing a room, of course—as two single male guests down from Cambridge, that was only to be expected, and such good pals as we were. I kept Morgan awake long into our first night, the Thursday, talking about his lovely soon-to-be fiancée, his future hopes, and present frustrations. Young gentlemen at that time did not talk openly about sex, not even to their bosom buddies and rowing pals, but Morgan came as close as he could without naming the parts—and it was enough for me to learn that he was as horny as a twenty-year-old athlete can be. At lunch that fateful (as it was to prove) Friday, I made sure that Morgan drank a little more Hock than he might have intended; he was thirsty, and I told him that there was nothing like a cold glass of white wine to set a chap up.

And so we found ourselves in a stuffy cupboard, two slightly drink-fuddled young men, pressed against each other in an attempt to evade detection by the hunting team. To close the cupboard door, it had been necessary for Morgan to wrap his long legs around me in the most awkward (but, to me, delightful) posture. Once inside, we could maneuver a little, and somehow Morgan ended up straddling me as I half-sat, half-lay, my back propped against a pile of picnic blankets. In this position it was easy for me to get my arm trapped—oh, how casually! How accidentally!—between his thigh and my waist. In working it free, with many a push, and a shove, and another push, and another, my hand came to rest over his groin. To Morgan's surprise, but not to mine, the contact and pressure had brought him to near erection.

"Hey, Boy," I whispered, "there's little enough room in here without you taking up space with that thing!" I gave his cock a squeeze through his blue flannels, just to make it clear what I was talking about. (Although he was a student of medicine, and thus of anatomy, Morgan was sometimes slow on the uptake in these matters.)

"I don't know what's wrong with me," he said—and I was delighted to hear that, though whispering, he was genuinely hoarse with embarrassment and desire.

"It must be the heat," I said.

"That's it. The heat..."

"And maybe the wine?"

"Oh, yes. Certainly the wine."

He shifted his hips around, but couldn't get up or off me. Not that he wanted to, I think, for in moving his hips he pressed his lengthening prick harder into my hand, and moved everything forward a few inches in so doing. Now he was positioned on my rib cage; it's a good thing I'm a strong, thickset Bostonian, or I'd have been crushed by those rower's thighs.

"Hell," I said, "feels like you've got an iron bar down there." I was taking a risk in referring so directly to his cock, but I counted on the Hock having done its work. And it had; Morgan was unused to wine, particularly at lunchtime, and seemed happy with the turn the conversation was taking. Even then, I dared not push my luck; one false move and my long-sought quarry would bolt, heedless of Sardine hunters.

"It's so uncomfortable in here," he said, wriggling around even more. To an experienced hand like me, the bucking movement of his hips suggested an urgent need for sexual release. I, of course, was stiff as a pole myself, had been ever since we climbed into the cupboard. I tilted my pelvis upward a little.

"Maybe if you leaned back a bit," I whispered. It worked like a charm. In lowering himself, Morgan achieved two things. First, he brought his butt into contact with my groin, and by the muffled gasp I could only assume that he figured out what was grinding into his coccyx. Second, he pressed his own cock even more painfully against the restricting fabric of his trousers.

"Oh, God..." It was half a whisper, half a moan.

"Here," I said, staking my all on this endgame, "let me make you a little more comfortable." With my free hand, I started unbuttoning his fly; he did nothing to resist. When I finally fished him out into the open, he seemed to relax, sighing and sinking backward. I got the impression that he'd finally figured out what all those nights in the pub, those naked swimming sessions, had really been about. I raised my knees to provide him with the support of my thighs; again, I thanked all those hours of training in gyms and boats.

As soon as his cock was out in the open, I knew he was mine for the taking. He wasn't yet fully erect; that would come when I got to work. For now I just let his prick rest in the palm of my hand, and I blew gently on it. Feeling the cool movement of the air, it jumped like a freshly landed catfish. My mouth watered.

"Shift your fat ass," I said. (Morgan always found my Americanisms amusing, and repeated them when we dined.) His ass was far from fat—in fact it resembled nothing more than a brace of cantaloupe melons—but he did as he was told. He struggled upward and allowed me to scoot out from beneath him, creating a racket of banging and bumping which should have alerted any sharp ears in the vicinity. Fortunately for us, there were none.

Now I had him. He was kneeling, sitting back on his heels, his cock sticking straight up in the air. By dint of crushing myself painfully against a pile of croquet hoops, I managed to get my head down to the right level. His prick was three inches from my lips.... I inhaled deeply, savoring the last moment of the hunt, the last moments of Morgan's innocence. Two inches... I opened my mouth, ready to receive him. One inch... I allowed my tongue to extend a little, tasting the first tentative contact with his glans.... And with that first, featherlight contact, an electric thrill passed through his body and into mine. He drew breath, fast and sharp. Had he sobered up too soon? And then, with one long exhalation, he sighed.

"Oh, yes..." His hands, warm and damp, moved onto my head, caressing my short-cropped brown hair.

And then, as I closed the gap between us and prepared to take Morgan's cock places it had never been before (specifically the back of my throat), the air was rent by a bloodcurdling scream.

We froze, the head of his cock resting on my lower lip, a drip of precum, unattended, gathering on my tongue.

"What was..."

He had no time to finish the question. Again, closer this time—a scream of horror and despair, the sound of feet running, heavy breathing, the panting of hysteria.

Reluctantly I relinquished Morgan's cock, stuffed him back into his pants and burst out of the cupboard, leaving him to fumble with his buttons in the gloom.

And there, standing at the head of the stairs, her hands clutched in her blonde hair in an attitude of crazed terror, her eyes wide and wet and her mouth open to scream again, stood the young heiress, Boy Morgan's fiancée, Belinda Eagle.

My first thought, quickly dismissed, was that she had somehow witnessed my lips closing around the head of her boyfriend's dick. That was impossible; there were no spy holes in English country houses, except in sensational novels, and besides, the initial scream had come from some yards away, possibly from a nearby landing.

Confident that my misdeeds remained undiscovered, I slipped immediately into Gallant American mode.

"Why, Miss Belinda," I said, still tasting Boy Morgan's salty precum where it had pooled on my tongue, "whatever is the matter?"

She looked at me, her pale blue eyes vacant, the pupils tiny. Was she, I wondered for a moment, a secret society cocaine fiend, such as I had read about in station waiting rooms?

Her mouth worked for a moment, but no sound came; I hoped, for the sake of my ears, that she wouldn't scream again.

"He's..."

"Yes?"

"Oh, God, he's..."

What? Queer? About to get his dick sucked? Hung like a horse? Begging for it? "What, Belinda? He's what?"

"He's..."

By this time Morgan had rebuttoned his fly, done a decent (but far from perfect) job of concealing his engorgement, and staggered out of our cupboard.

"Belinda! My darling!"

At the sight of her sweetheart, Belinda's terror melted into something much more manageable. "Oh, Harry!" She teetered toward him. "He's...dead!" And with that she fainted into his arms in a tableau worthy of the London stage.

Within moments, Drekeham Hall was in uproar. No sooner had Belinda made her swooning confession than the place was swarming with policemen, who poured into the lobby from every direction. Now, I enjoyed plays in the West End during my occasional trips to the capital, particularly farces, and was always mightily amused by the speed with which the bobby appeared on the scene the moment the crime had been committed. I never imagined, however, that this was based on actual fact. But there before my very eyes was living, running proof of the uncanny efficiency of the British police force. Three came through the front door, two from the stairs that led to the kitchens, two from the direction of the park and garden. They converged on the decorative inlay that formed an intricate design of concentric circles and stars on the hall floor (all Italian marble; Sir James Eagle was a man of substance). Of all this I had a bird's-eye view, poised on the landing and peering down through the railings.

Sir James himself strode out of his study and straight up to what I took to be the senior cop.

"Officer," he said, in the same tones with which he regularly quelled an unruly House of Commons, "there has been an appalling accident."

"Sir?" The officer did not seem particularly surprised.

"A young man has been found in the most distressing circumstances."

"Dead, Sir James?"

"Dead, sergeant."

"His name, sir?"

Sir James seemed to hesitate for a moment, and then: "Reginald Walworth. Known as Reg, I believe."

"A guest, Sir James?"

"Yes. A guest in Drekeham Hall. It's appalling. Really most appalling..." He shaded his eyes with a hand and turned his back on the Greek chorus of seven policemen. It looked, at first, like a well-rehearsed gesture of grief—and yet I could see, from my vantage point, that Sir James's features were distorted in genuine distress. His eyes were screwed up as if he was in pain; he grimaced as if he had just taken some very nasty medicine. He breathed deeply to compose himself, stared heavenward—and caught my gaze, looking straight down into his eyes. Sir James Eagle, MP, was in his forties—once himself a Cambridge Rowing Blue, and still, despite the lines etched deeply in his face by public office, a handsome man. Catching my puzzled expression, he turned on his heel and addressed the police.

"The body is in my study, gentlemen, where it...he...was found. Would you follow me?"

"Certainly, sir."

And with that, the entire squadron marched up the stairs with Sir James at the head, the sergeant at his heels, the rest in pairs behind. I backed up against the wall to let them pass, asking myself if all country-house murders went off with such precision drilling. (I was not so perplexed, however, that I did not notice that at least two of the policemen, including the sergeant, were good-looking, and that at least four of them gave me an appraising glance as they passed me on the landing. I must have still been bulging.)

The procession disappeared down a corridor—in the direction, I guessed, from which we first heard Belinda scream. I longed to follow them, to penetrate this mystery, but decorum held me back. Even in America, we don't barge in on personal tragedy, and I knew only too well that any display of inquisitiveness would be frostily repelled at Drekeham Hall.

And yet my curiosity was piqued—so much that I had almost forgotten Boy Morgan, who had laid his beloved out on the carpet and was now hopping from one foot to the other, his cock giving him some discomfort. Youth and athleticism are a wonderful combination: not even a sudden murder can quell the storm in a young man's flannels.

Now, I was caught between a rock and, quite literally, a hard place. You will understand that part of me wanted nothing more than to take advantage of the hubbub in the house, lure Morgan off to our bedroom, and spend the rest of the afternoon fucking his brains out. But there was another part of me that wanted to find out what was really going on in the dressing room of Sir James Eagle, MP—and to understand that, you must know a little more about me.

As a child in Boston, growing up in comfortable affluence with my merchant father and heiress mother, I, Edward Mitchell, became addicted to detective fiction. It was my first love. At the age of seven, I read Conan Doyle's *A Study in Scarlet*, and from there I devoured every Sherlock Holmes story in the bookstores. By scouring our public libraries, I discovered more: G. K. Chesterton, Wilkie Collins, and a new English writer of promise, Agatha Christie. Of course, I remained faithful to Doyle—but, as I grew to manhood and spent more time at my studies or sporting activities, I found that I could relax with anything that came to hand, no matter how trashy. Serial publications were readily available for a few cents—and, if it had a corpse and a cop, I was the first in line to buy the new number, which I would devour whole in my bed at night (unless I had company, when that was devoured whole instead).

And so you will understand why little Teddy Mitchell grew up with a burning desire to be a private detective. Like Doyle, I was a student of medicine—and, I flattered myself, I had an eye for the telling forensic detail. I also had a nose for hypocrisy, and an instinct for divining the truths of human motivation. This, perhaps, I had acquired in my late teens, when I discovered that the offices, drawing rooms, public libraries, and sporting facilities of middle-class Boston were home to activities that would have made the Revolutionary Fathers blush. My first important lover was a prominent Boston businessman—he was twice my age, but that didn't stop us from fucking each other silly at every opportunity for a period of nearly three years. And under his welcome tutelage I discovered pleasure almost wherever I looked. I was shameless, and handsome, and well-endowed, and those three things in combination, I think, will never leave you high and dry.

To cut a long story short, as a twenty-two-year-old postgraduate medical student, I was ruled by two passions: cock and crime. And here, at Drekeham Hall, both were being offered to me. Which would I choose?

One I was fairly sure would keep for a while: Morgan was certainly going to get no satisfaction from the inert form of his sweetheart, and had sampled enough of what I had to offer to bring him back for more. As for the other—I knew from my extensive reading that the very worst mistake a sleuth can make is to let the trail go cold. Gather evidence while it's fresh, and you stand a much better chance of finding the one clue that has evaded everyone else—and that will lead to your solution.

With that in mind, I proceeded down the corridor, hellbent on eavesdropping—but not before I had insured my later pleasure by marching over to Morgan, pushing him against the paneled wall of the landing, grabbing his still-surging groin, and kissing him full on the mouth. It was an act of bravado I would never have ventured under normal circumstances, but somehow the scent of murder had emboldened me. He neither recoiled nor struck me—he simply stood there, his mouth hanging open, a strand of saliva (his? mine?) hanging from his lower lip, a glazed look in his eye—confused, perhaps, by the taste of his own cock in my mouth.

Yes, he would keep, all right.

No sooner had I rounded the corner, still smiling after my successful assault on Boy Morgan, than I was accosted by a sinister presence that materialized, apparently, out of nowhere. I say "sinister" perhaps with the benefit of hindsight. But no, there really was something sinister about Leonard

Eagle, Sir James's brother, the troublesome youngest of this brood of Eagles. He had the ravaged looks of a man twice his age; though only thirty-five, his face was lined with experience, and his eyes gave new meaning to the word *knowing*. He was exceptionally slender—one would have said skinny, were it not for the fact that he offset his thin frame with an extraordinary poise and elegance that rendered him curiously compelling to both men and women. He wore his hair longer than was the norm in those days, brushed back off his forehead and curling around the nape of his neck. His clothes were elegant—too elegant, some would say, for his tailor had tapered his waistline to emphasize Leonard's epicene silhouette, and had satisfied his client's taste for color in a lining of crimson figured silk. Add to that a pair of exquisitely manicured, bejeweled hands, a cloud of intoxicating scent, and you had Leonard Eagle—vampirelike, beautiful, just this side of effeminate. It was whispered that Leonard was an "embarrassment" to his upright older brother, from whom he sponged shamelessly and upon whose influence he relied to keep him out of trouble. His nephew Rex, Boy Morgan, and the rest of the "hearties" dismissed him as an awful aesthete and waster; I was both intrigued and repulsed.

Leonard Eagle glided noiselessly on soft leather shoes, took me by the elbow with one soft hand, and guided me to the head of the stairs—in the opposite direction from my pursuit of the police.

"Terrible business, we're so sorry," he whispered, his full red mouth a little too close to my ear. "We hope our guests won't be too upset." I tried to stop in my tracks, but he was surprisingly strong. "Mama suggested I take you round the gardens, show you the horses, that sort of thing."

"Well, if you don't mind, I..."

"So distressing for Lady Caroline, all of this."

"Yes..."

What could I do? I could not distress Mother Eagle any

further. And so I allowed Leonard to steer me downstairs—but not before I had noticed, along the corridor where the police procession had trooped, an open cupboard door, just like the one behind which I had so recently tasted Boy Morgan's juice. And from that open cupboard spilled an odd assortment of boots, newspapers, and tennis balls, as if something had been pulled hastily from within, bringing with it a random selection of contents.

Something—or someone.

I was still looking over my shoulder, trying to note any further clues, when Leonard Eagle commanded all my attention with a few simple words.

"You seem to be getting on very nicely with Boy Morgan."

I'm not easily fazed, and kept my cool despite the note of insinuation in his voice. Had someone, after all, been watching us?

"Yes," I said, with exaggerated heartiness, "Morgan's a good man. He's been a great pal at Cambridge."

"I'm sure..." His voice was laden with insinuation, but I wasn't going to rise to the bait. "I had great pals at Cambridge too...." I could play the bluff Yank as well as anyone—and, after all, Leonard had no reason to suspect my true nature, which expressed itself so differently from his. (So indiscreet had Leonard been with his "great pals" that, rumor had it, he'd been expelled.) To the casual observer, I was every inch the College Jock—a pose that got me far more cock than any obvious display of effeminacy. I wondered how it worked for Leonard, who had the feline contentment of a man well fucked.

He whisked me down the stairs, across the hall, and into the small reception room that led to the garden. I had the distinct impression that I was being got out of the way.

Then, for a moment, in this elegant little room with its painted panels and Turkish carpets, cool and shady despite the heat of the day, we stopped. "But," continued Leonard, "do you think Boy Morgan is really quite right for my niece?"

Not if I have anything to do with it, I thought; by the end of the weekend I intended to get Boy Morgan hopelessly addicted to dick.

"In what sense, exactly?"

Leonard looked me up and down—I knew that kind of glance all too well from the back streets of Beacon Hill. He paused, took my elbow again, and led me through the French doors and onto the terrace. "I don't know," he said airily, guiding our steps toward the lawn, yet further from the house. "He strikes me as...well, you know."

"He strikes me as a thoroughly good chap." This kind of meaningless Anglicism sounded even more hollow with a Boston twang.

"Thoroughly good, of course," drawled Leonard. "Solid, you might say."

What had he seen? Nothing, surely...

"And yet..."

"Yes?"

We cleared the patio and strode across the lawn toward the woods; by now Leonard had slipped his arm through mine.

"Yet I wonder if he's not just a little..."

"Mmmm?" I wasn't going to give him the satisfaction, even for a moment, of understanding his hints.

"I don't know. Just a little...dull. Belinda's a lively girl."

"They seem very much in love." Damn it all, they did.

"Oh, yes, she's in love with him. Who wouldn't be? He's absolutely charming...to look at." Leonard glanced sideways to see how I responded.

"Certainly, he's a fine man."

"Ye-e-es..."

"A good man."

"Is he indeed?"

It was time to put an end to these insinuations. I stopped, disengaged my arm, and turned to face my unwanted companion. He was smiling—a vague, distant smile that he probably thought sphinxlike.

"I would rather not discuss my friends with...comparative strangers," I said. "Now, if you don't mind, I shall go to my room."

Leonard laughed. "Come on, old chap, there's no need to go all puritanical on me," he said. "The house is in a miserable state, crawling with ghastly policemen, it's a beautiful day, and I intend to show you the grounds. Now," he said, taking my arm once again, "you wouldn't deprive your host of the pleasure of showing a guest round his grounds, would you? Especially such delightful grounds as mine, and such a presentable guest as you."

He had me figured out all right—the only mystery was how. I allowed myself to be led; odious he may have been, but there was something hypnotic about Leonard Eagle.

We walked through the formal gardens toward a rustic retaining wall, beyond which the garden turned into park, then woods, then cliff. "Beautiful, isn't it?" sighed Leonard, holding tightly to my arm. "I only appreciate it when I see it through the eyes of a visitor. Otherwise I suppose I take it for granted."

"I imagine you spend a good deal of your time in town, Mr. Eagle."

"I do, Mr. Mitchell, but hang it, I shan't call you that, nor shall you call me Mr. Eagle. It's Leonard if you must, or Lennie to the family, and I shan't tell you what my close friends call me, or at least not until I know you a good deal better. What shall I call you? Edward? Teddy? Edwina?"

"Mitch will do." This was what my Cambridge friends called me. (Only my mother was allowed to call me Teddy.)

"I'm sure you've been called many other things...."

"Meaning?"

"Oh, terms of endearment by sweethearts, of which you must have swooning legions in Cambridge and—where is it? Baltimore?"

"Boston, Mr. Eagle."

"Boston, of course. And do you?"

"Do I what?"

"Have sweethearts?"

"I do not."

"Or...particular friendships?"

"I have many friendships."

"Of that I am sure."

He caught my eye and we held each other's gaze. There was little doubting his intentions. To my shame, I was flattered and aroused.

"Now," he said, switching to a tone of breezy camaraderie, "we can ride, or bathe, or play tennis, as you wish."

"It's far too hot for tennis or riding."

"And bathing, Mitch?"

"I wouldn't object."

"Then follow me!"

He took off with amazing speed across the park, leaping over hummocks like a prancing deer. He lingered at the entrance to the woods—waiting, not even beckoning. I followed—faster and more powerful than him, but less agile, tripping occasionally on an unexpected root. Just as I caught up with him he disappeared from view.

I blundered into the woods, blinded by the change from sunshine to shadow, out of breath and horribly hot. The air in there was cool, and I had a terrible urge to shuck off my country-house clothes.

"Mr. Eagle?" I called. "Leonard? Lennie?"

No reply but the crack of a twig and the pale outline of a figure darting further into the woods. I followed, acutely conscious of the blood rushing in my ears.

A circle of ancient rhododendrons, long past their prime, stood thick and funereal in what might otherwise have been a pleasant, airy clearing. How typical, I thought, of English gardeners to "improve" nature with their gruesome imports. And then, the last thing I expected to hear—the trickle of water. Somewhat behind me and to my right, a hesitant stream ran through the woods, straight into the heart of the dark clump of evergreens. I approached, expectant.

The outer ring of rhododendrons was several feet thick, but, by stooping, I found a perfect tunnel, easily passable—and there, on the other side, surrounded by a mulch of fallen leaves, was a round, gleaming pool of water.

And in its center was exactly what I expected to see—the naked floating form of Leonard Eagle.

"Come and join me!" he said, splashing great ropes of diamonds loose through the sunny air. "Nobody else ever comes here. They've all forgotten about it apart from me." I looked cautiously around, and saw his clothes hanging neatly on a branch—including his underwear. "I never bother with bathing togs. Don't worry. We won't be interrupted."

The heat of the day, the excitement of my interlude in the cupboard—not to mention the proximity of a real-life murder—predisposed me to bathing. But I must confess to a further inducement: Leonard Eagle's pale, sculpted neck, shoulders, and chest, glistening with fresh, cold water, looked too good to ignore.

I was out of my jacket, shirt, and tie in seconds. The air felt so good on my skin that all the hair on my chest, stomach, and arms stood on end for a moment. I glanced over to Leonard, whose eyes widened. I guessed that his languid London friends had neither the athletic build nor the dark pelt with which nature had endowed me. I stood for a moment and stretched my arms above my head; I knew, from the remarks of previous admirers and from my own evenings in front of the mirror, that this position showed off my torso to good effect. To my delight, Leonard looked completely discountenanced; muscles such as mine were a rare sight in England in 1925, where "strong men" were confined to circus tents and music halls.

I fixed his gaze for a moment, lifted an eyebrow, and proceeded to kick off my shoes, peel off my socks, and unbutton my trousers. Leonard had adopted a position floating on his back, in which it was quite easy to discern that he was completely naked, and considerably aroused. It has always been my experience that skinny men of wolfish appearance have huge pricks, and Leonard confirmed my findings.

I took time with my trousers, folded them carefully, and added them to a little pile on a patch of dry leaves. Now I stood up in my underpants—and they weren't doing a lot to disguise the fact that I was playing the same game as Leonard. I'm easily turned on, and, despite my reservations about Leonard's motives in leading me down the garden path, I wasn't going to turn down a chance to fuck a family member.

I stepped out of my pants and stood, fully erect, on the edge of the pool. Leonard was as shameless as me; we were well matched in that respect. His cock, as long as mine but not as thick, was breaking the surface by several inches. Ripples broke around it like waves around a lighthouse.

I waded up to my knees, then dived forward and down, submerging my head, kicking up my heels, and swimming a few strokes underwater. The cool wetness felt great, and for a moment I forgot everything but the sensation. Then I opened my eyes, looked through the greenish murk and saw Leonard Eagle's legs bending and flexing above me. I swam upward, straight between them, launched myself on top of his body, and grasped him in my arms. He must have thought for a moment that I intended to drown him, as his eyes widened in shock—but I clamped my mouth over his, flipped onto my back, and, kicking my legs frog-fashion, carried us both safely to shallow water. There we lay, kissing like starving men, his smooth, sinuous, white body pressed down onto my dark, hairy, stocky form, our two wet cocks slipping and flipping beside each other in mute combat.

I knew from the first moment I saw him that Leonard was vicious, but nothing had prepared me for the dexterity with which he conducted our coupling. Within a minute of grappling like this, he had maneuvered himself into a straddling position, and was cranking my cock like the starting handle of a car. The look on his face, as he stared down at me, showed that he knew exactly what he wanted and how to get it. He spat on his hand, transferred the saliva to his backside and worked it well in; I could tell the exact moment when his finger entered his body, as he gasped a little, and his eyes took on a glazed, reptilian quality. When he looked down again, there was strange fire sparkling in his green irises.

I raised my hips out of the water and braced myself to take his weight. Leonard adjusted his position with the precision of a seasoned fuckee, placed my fat bulbous head against his sphincter, and then engulfed me. I had never been taken like that before. There was no pushing, no resistance, no grunting or struggling as had so often been the case with male lovers. Instead his ass opened like a mouth to draw me inside, capturing me with a tight, warm wetness. And then began the fuck; I could hardly say that I fucked him, as all I could do was tense my muscles and hold myself in position. Leonard's body hardly moved, but the vacuum inside him was playing merry hell with my cock. It seemed as if a hundred hands, a hundred mouths, were working on me; pressures and textures rippled around my shaft, setting my balls boiling like potatoes in a saucepan. Under the surface of his milky white, tight skin I could see the muscles of his abdomen and thighs working in subtle, sinuous rhythms—and all the while that gold fire in the eyes. The only thing over which he had no control was his own prick, which jerked and throbbed with every inner squeeze. Drops of nectar gathered at the head and ran down like wax on a candle. It was too much to resist; I grabbed his cock, scooped up as much juice as I could, and brought it to my mouth. My second taste of the day, and just as delicious as the first.

Leonard was grinning down at me with a look that said *I told you so*. I was too far gone to resent it; instead I grabbed him by the upper arm, pulled him toward me and made him kiss me. Perhaps it was the taste of his own juice in my mouth, perhaps it was the changed angle of the fucking as he was pulled forward—for whatever reason, he reached the point of no return. His cock, trapped between his white, ridged stomach and my solid, hairy one, gave one almighty twitch and let fly with a huge jet of spunk. For a moment we were stuck together—while, around us in the water, floated white globs of sperm.

I was ready to shoot my load inside him, such was the intensity of the ride—but Leonard had other ideas.

He jumped up, ejecting my cock from his ass like a train from a tunnel—which must have hurt, I remember thinking. And then, barely rinsing my dick in the cold water of the pool, he swallowed it whole. His mouth was looser and less exquisitely rippling than his backside, but it only took one look down at his soaked hair, his pale face and sparkling eyes—not to mention his lips stretched wide around my tool—and I was giving it to him right down the back of his throat.

We lay together, the water lapping our overheated bodies, the sun broken by the gently moving leaves of the surrounding bushes, and I must have dozed off. Certainly it came as a shock when the body next to mine suddenly tensed and shifted. I opened my eyes, took a moment to realize where I was and with whom, and saw Leonard springing to his feet like a cat stalking a bird. There was the distant sound of a slamming door, of feet crunching on gravel...at least, so I thought. The house was hundreds of yards off. I couldn't be sure of what I heard.

Leonard, however, seemed satisfied. He was dressing now, rubbing the moisture from his body with his shirt, climbing into his trousers. With his shoes and socks in one hand, he padded through the bushes toward the house—without a word of farewell, a kiss, even a caress. This struck me as strange from one who, only a moment ago, was riding my dick to glory.

"Wait," I said. "I'll come with you."

He looked down at me, the sun behind his head. Was that a sneer I saw on his face? And then, turning on a heel, he disappeared from view.

II

BACK AT THE HOUSE, ORDER HAD BEEN RESTORED. THE police had gone, the inner rooms were quiet, there was not a soul to be seen—in fact, you'd never know that within the last hour a dead body had been dragged out of a closet by a hysterical young woman.

It dawned on me that Leonard's efficient seduction had been a calculated ruse to get me out of the house while whatever had to be done was done, without the inconvenience of witnesses. I cursed myself for my stupidity, for allowing lust to cloud my judgment; I felt like the typical naive, trusting New Worlder, caught in the snares of a scheming European. They would not trick me so easily again, not even with slim white bodies and man-eating anuses.

I strolled across the silent hall and took the stairs two at a time. There was the cupboard in which I had frolicked with Boy Morgan, now closed and empty. And there, along the landing, was the cupboard which, so recently, I had seen in disarray—and it, too, was as tidy as if nothing had happened. It seemed as if an army of housemaids had worked their way through the house with the speed of lightning, leaving no trace of recent disruptions. If only I had been able to examine the evidence while it was fresh! But no: I had followed my prick instead. What would Sherlock Holmes have said?

I knelt by the cupboard and looked all around it, at the wood of the door, at the paint, at the carpet in front, hoping to find a smear of blood, a sign of struggle, something that would lead me onward in what I now called my "investigation." But it was hopeless; there was nothing. At least, nothing I could see. I cursed Sherlock Holmes for his smug sure-footedness; it always seemed so easy on the printed page. And here was "Mitch" Mitchell, would-be detective, who didn't even know the identity of the victim. This would have to be remedied.

I was about to make my way into the study across the passage which I knew to be occupied by Sir James Eagle, and where the body had been presented to the police; I would blunder in, pretending to be lost, and see what I could see. The worst they could do was ask me, in that polite British way, to leave; the rules of hospitality would prevent worse.

My hand was practically on the doorknob when I heard a hissing noise from a few feet away. I halted, waited, and heard it again. I turned, and there was the ashen face of Boy Morgan appearing around the corner, beckoning me to follow. Surely he wasn't that desperate for me to suck him off? I had allowed sex to get in the way of my investigations once that day; I wouldn't let it happen again. I turned, and was about to enter Sir James's study, when Morgan called me.

"Mitch, for God's sake. Please!"

He sounded in distress, rather than extreme sexual arousal, and I never could resist a friend in need.

"What's up?"

"It's Belinda. She...she says she saw something. I can't

get any sense out of the girl, Mitch, but I'm frightened. Something's happened here."

His close-set eyes were pleading. It was a prospect that I found altogether delightful; the young athletic hero trembling before me, begging for assistance.

I laid a hand on his broad rower's shoulder and squeezed. "Calm down, Morgan. I'm here now."

"Thank God." Then he did something that I had only ever seen girls do before: he fell into my arms. I was taken aback, but I held him nonetheless. I could feel his chest working with emotion. My embrace seemed to calm him, so I ventured a small kiss on the side of his neck—the sort of kiss that might just be explained away as a gesture of quasi-familial affection. His neck tasted delicious, of soap and sweat.

Morgan didn't break from my grasp—in fact, he seemed content to hang there for a while, resting his head on my shoulder. And so I tried another kiss, more definite this time, and another. I moved my mouth upward to his jawline—a jawline so firm and elegant that I had longed to kiss it from the moment we'd met. This time Morgan let his head hang back, offering his throat to my mouth. I felt certain that we would be surprised at any moment, but neither of us cared, nor was able to stop. I kissed again, with real passion this time, the heat surging back into my groin, and pushed him against the wall. Our cocks crushed against each other.

For a moment, I broke for air and looked him square in the face. He had the puzzled look of a man utterly in the grip of desire; I had seen it often enough to recognize the signs. His mouth was hanging open—to be honest, he looked somewhat imbecilic at that moment—so I kissed him there. This time he returned the kiss with equal, if not greater, passion.

"I can't stand it," he said, when we took a breather. "I've got to come right away."

There was a bathroom just along the landing; Drekeham Hall, unusually for the day, was lavishly equipped with sanitary facilities. And so I pushed him in there, bolted the door, and continued my assault on his face. He grabbed my hand and pushed it down, straight onto his hard, naked cock. He wasn't exaggerating: within three or four strokes the thing was jumping in my hand like a motorized banana, and before I had time to step back a great long spurt of sperm had shot onto my trousers. Unwilling to see such natural bounty go to waste, I quickly dropped to a crouching position and took shots two, three, and four in my mouth. I'm sure that, under normal circumstances, Boy would have been horrified at the idea of coming in another man's mouth (whereas mutual masturbation, for young men of his class, was not entirely unknown). Still, the poor soul was so far gone in lust that he registered only the sensation—for the time being, at least. I was delighted: I'd got the prize, and I savored every drop.

Boy was in a sort of orgasmic delirium for a while, his eyes closed, his head thrown back, exposing that beautiful column of a neck. I took the opportunity to nurse on his cock for a while, and only after I had sucked out the last of his spunk did he start to soften. As the blood flowed back to his brain, he turned back into the rather formal young man I had worked so hard to corrupt.

"Good lord..." he started, then thought better of going on, because he was not yet so accustomed to vice that he could frame the words "you swallowed my load." But I could read his mind; this was something that, generally speaking, didn't happen to well-bred young men in 1925. At least, not with their girlfriends.

I thought it best to get things back onto a businesslike footing, and once I had relinquished his cock from my mouth (it made a satisfying plop as it left) I stood up and began to sponge Boy Morgan's jizz from my flannels. I stood with my back to the door; I didn't want him bolting just yet, even though I could see from his flustered expression that he wanted to.

There was a moment's silence, during which I'm sure he was struggling to make some kind of pronouncement. It could have gone either way. Would it be "Mr. Mitchell, what we have just done is wrong and disgusting and if you ever speak of it to a soul I will horsewhip you"? Or would it be a more tender declaration? I hoped for the latter, but couldn't bear the former, so I spoke first.

"So, Boy, you were saying something about Belinda."

His fiancée's name jerked Boy back to reality, and he hurriedly stuffed his cock back into his pants, away from my hungry eyes.

"Yes," he said, then had to clear his throat. "Er...yes. She's not making a lot of sense. She thinks she saw something."

At last—some evidence. Mitch Mitchell, postgraduate detective, sprung into action.

"Then," I said, "I had better talk to her. Lead on, Mr. Morgan."

I stood aside and allowed him to open the door. He stuck his head out, gingerly checking that there was nobody to witness two young men coming out of a bathroom that was only designed for single occupancy. While he was doing so, I took the opportunity to bump against his rear—ever so casually and accidentally, but with sufficient force that he would feel the big hard bulge against his ass. It was worth reminding him, when vulnerable, that we still had unfinished business. He moved away—eventually. Oh, I thought, roll on bedtime.

Belinda Eagle was everything a young man of the 1920s could desire. She was blonde and slender, but without attaining the entirely boyish silhouette to which many of her sisters aspired. (And I knew from late-night conversations with many of my Cambridge friends that they mourned the absence of tits from their female contemporaries.) She was fashionably turned out, with shingled hair and a drop-waisted dress, but she had not abandoned the art of feminine frivolity that attracted male attention. She was as fresh and fragrant as a spring morning, and as artless as an angel. If there were one person in the Eagle family who could be trusted, it was surely Belinda.

She had rallied well from her earlier hysterics, and was sitting at her dressing table combing her hair when Boy Morgan ushered me in. I hoped that the semen stains on my flannels were not too obvious, and thanked my strictly hygienic upbringing for obliging me to wash my hands after touching cock. She took my proffered hand—the very one that had brought her boyfriend to climax—and motioned me to a chair. Boy lounged on the bed, paying scant attention to what we said; his mind was elsewhere.

"Well," Belinda said, in the jolly, sporty tones that made her such a favorite with the boys, "what a dreadful affair!"

I knew from my reading of detective fiction that it was sometimes wise to let a witness run on a little at first.

"Dreadful indeed, Miss Eagle."

"Whoever would have thought it?"

"Thought what, exactly?"

"Well, that we had a murderer in our midst. It's too scared-making!"

"It is."

"Still, we can all rest easy in our beds now, thank goodness. The police have their man."

This was the first I had heard of an arrest. Little wonder that Leonard was so eager to distance me from the house in the aftermath of the crime. I thought it best to play dumb.

"Thank God for that. Who did it?"

"It was Meeks. Isn't that ghastly?"

"Meeks, Miss Eagle?"

"The first footman. Such a quiet chap. I would never have thought it possible."

"Which one is Meeks?" Despite having been in England for a couple of years, I could still not distinguish between the ranks of "indoor staff."

"Oh, you know, pale-faced character with a little Vandyke beard. Never says boo to a goose."

I knew immediately whom she meant, and had already admired the first footman's tactful efficiency at the table— not to mention a beautifully rounded pair of buttocks that his short jacket and tailored trousers showed to good advantage. I like a nice backside on a man, and had noted with delight the fact that, for a man of slight build, the first footman nevertheless had something to sit upon. That aside, I had paid him little attention, being hell-bent on corrupting Boy Morgan.

"And it was him?"

"Apparently so."

"He's under arrest?"

"Yes. He didn't deny it, either. The police took him away without a struggle. Isn't it extraordinary? Just think, all that time, when he was serving the soup, or clearing away, or bringing one tea, he was scheming a foul crime like that."

It was time, I decided, to do a little circuitous investigation.

"And how is the rest of the family taking it?"

"Oh, we're all terribly shocked of course, but Mummy and Daddy are bearing up. They're a great support to each other. As for Rex... Well, it's quite wonderful, really..."

"Yes?"

"He's just carrying on as if nothing had happened at all. That's typical of my brother; he's such a very serious chap. No sooner had all this blown up than he was off on some business trip to London that was frightfully important and couldn't wait another minute. Said he'd intended to go anyway, though it was the first I'd heard of it, mind you that's nothing new, he never tells me anything."

I noticed Boy's eyebrows were raised; evidently he knew nothing of it either, and he thought himself a great pal of Belinda's older brother.

"Well good for him for not letting anything get in the way of business," I said. "Evidently he wasn't upset by this little incident."

Belinda frowned for a minute. "I wouldn't exactly say that," she said, weighing her words and glancing up to see how much I was taking in. "He was...well, I heard him and Daddy..."

"What, Miss Belinda?" I usually found that if I turned on the American charm it worked wonders, particularly with English girls.

"They were having the most frightful row, if you must know. Then Rex came storming out of Daddy's study with a face like thunder, and got Hibbert to drive him to the station. I only had time for the quickest of words...."

"And you'd heard nothing of this business trip before?"

"Not a sausage."

"London's a long way to go on a whim."

"I don't think Rex really has whims, Mr. Mitchell."

"Please call me Mitch. Everyone else does. Eh, Boy?" I prodded Boy with my toe; he was off in a reverie, possibly not unconnected with what he'd felt pressing into his backside. He was, unlike me, incapable of holding two thoughts at once.

"Rather..." he said, vaguely.

"Does your brother have many friends in London, Miss Belinda?"

"I suppose he must know oodles of people. I mean, one does. And of course now he's working...." Rex Eagle had, on graduating, taken a good position in the family import business, the profits from which had bought and maintained

Drekeham Hall and earned Sir James his knighthood.

"Funny to come all the way down here for just one night if he knew he had to dash up to town again so soon, though, isn't it? Heck of a long train ride."

"Yes...but I suppose that's business for you. Daddy says business must come first. I mean even Mummy daren't disturb Daddy when he's got business to attend to."

"Perhaps he's gone to see Whopper," Boy said, brightening suddenly.

"Don't be silly, Boy. Whopper's on her way here from Trouville, as you well know."

"Oh." He sank back into abstraction.

"Who's 'Whopper'?" I asked. I found the English fashion for absurd nicknames strangely irritating.

"Whopper Hunt. Rex's intended," explained Boy.

"Otherwise known as Lady Diana Hunt, daughter of the Earl of Newington, a great friend of Daddy's," Belinda said. "We called her Whopper at school because she was awfully good at hockey and used to whop the ball all the way down the pitch. You didn't want to get in the way when Whopper Hunt was on the warpath." Belinda rubbed her shins in memory of long-faded bruises. "Frightful girl at the time, but Daddy says she's got a good head on her shoulders. And Rex is terribly smitten."

"So they plan to marry?"

"Oh, yes! And I'm going to be chief bridesmaid! Well, at least, if Boy doesn't make an honest woman of me first, in which case I shall be matron of honor."

I wouldn't depend on your Boy turning out to be the marrying kind, I thought, and was instantly ashamed of my cruelty. Surely there was enough of Boy to share.

"Gosh, Belinda, don't embarrass Mitch."

"Come on, Boy, Mitch knows we're only waiting for your parents to get back from India..."

I was in no hurry to hear more about Boy Morgan's marriage plans, and steered the conversation back to Rex and his Valkyrie bride-to-be.

"How long have Rex and Diana been courting?"

"Oh, forever," Belinda said. "They were childhood sweethearts. She's the daughter of a super family in Lincolnshire, her father is terribly grand. We've always said they'd marry. Isn't that lovely? Something so real and pure and true that time itself couldn't change the way they feel."

I wondered if this remark was directed at Boy, who was shifting around on the bed as if eager to be off.

"Is Rex very much in love?"

Boy snorted.

"Well," Belinda said, casting him an angry look, "I wouldn't call Rex the romantic type. He doesn't go in for all that stuff. Nor does she. They're quite a modern couple in that respect. Very matter-of-fact."

It didn't sound like a particularly romantic union, and I suspected that business and dynastic interests may have been as important to serious Rex Eagle as any tender feelings. The sangfroid of the English upper classes never ceased to amaze me; when I was in love, nothing would come between me and the object of my desire.

"And Miss Hunt has been in France?"

"Yes. She goes over for the golf, I believe." Belinda smirked slightly; she obviously did not consider golf a particularly ladylike pursuit. "I pity any poor soul who gets in the way of her balls."

Boy shot me a look that absolutely forbade any jocular riposte.

"What an independent young lady she must be."

"That's Whopper for you."

This was getting me nowhere—though I couldn't help feeling that Sherlock Holmes would, by now, have picked out the vital clue from Belinda's disjointed narrative.

"Pardon my intrusion, Miss Belinda, but Boy mentioned

that you saw something earlier that...distressed you."

"Well," she said, with a hint of pride, "it was me that found him, you know."

"Indeed."

"Yes. I opened the cupboard and out he fell. I thought I was doing terrifically well, being a hunter and everything, and then I noticed that he was...well, dead."

"Yes. And that was when we found you."

"Thank heavens." She beamed at Boy, who blushed and nodded, ever the modest hero.

"Was there anything you noticed at the time that seemed...unusual?"

"Apart from finding a dead gentleman in the sports cupboard, you mean? Even in our house, Mr. Mitchell, that is not quite usual."

"I beg your pardon, Miss. I meant anything that struck you as peculiar?"

"Come on, Billie, tell Mitch what you told me."

"I don't know now, Boy. I think I may have been mistaken."

"What was it, Miss Belinda?"

"I thought I saw—but now I'm wondering if, after all, I'm getting confused with what happened when."

"Spit it out." Boy immediately blushed; I can't imagine what he was thinking of.

"Well, I have this distinct impression in my mind that I saw some tracks on the landing carpet," she said, "as if something had been dragged into the cupboard."

"I see," I said. "And where did the tracks come from?" Follow those tracks, I thought, and we're on the scent.

"But now I suppose what I must have seen was afterwards, when they'd taken the poor young man to Daddy's dressing room. I was in such a state that I didn't know what was what."

"Are you sure about that?"

"I suppose I must be."

"But Billie," Boy said, "that's not what you told me."

"This is terribly embarrassing, but I think I must have fainted and got muddled."

"Poor Billie," Boy said, standing up for the first time and putting a protective hand on his fragile fiancée's shoulder, "you've been through hell."

This was hopeless. My one big clue turned out to be nothing more than the muddled recollection of a woman whose evidence would be demolished in a court of law.

"And when you found the—the deceased," I asked, "was there anything to suggest the way in which he died? Any blood?"

"I say, Mitch, come on," Boy said. "Let's not distress poor Billie any more than is necessary. She's told you what she wanted to tell you."

"I'm sorry," I said, mentally promising myself that, when I finally got inside Boy Morgan's ass, I would be merciless. "I didn't mean to—"

Belinda rallied. "No, nothing of the gory sort," she said. "The police said that he had been throttled."

Boy stood between Belinda and me, as if to shield her. "My poor darling. How awful."

"I leave you, Miss Belinda, in the capable hands of your fiancé. Boy, I shall see you when we dress for dinner."

He caught my eye for a moment, then lowered his gaze to the floor. For all he was playing the knight in shining armor, I knew that I had found his chink, and I intended to work on that opening with every weapon in my arsenal.

III

WITH SEVERAL HOURS TO GO BEFORE DINNER, I SLIPPED out of the house and strolled into the village of Drekeham, nearly two miles along the cliffs and inland from the family seat of the Eagles. I was playing a hunch that, in the hurry to get Meeks out of the way, the police had taken the supposed murderer to the nearest secure unit—Drekeham Police Station. When I had seen it during a preliminary walk around the village on the day of my arrival, it seemed like a quiet sort of place where the biggest excitement might come from a dispute over grazing rights. Clearly, however, there was manpower enough within those walls to make a clean sweep of Drekeham Hall and to arrest a suspect—all in the time it took me to fuck Leonard Eagle.

I reported to the front desk and relied, as I had long since learned to do, on the British belief that all Americans were semicretins. The desk sergeant was, to my eyes, well past retirement age, and treated me with a lack of manners that was almost offensive.

"I am staying at Drekeham Hall," I announced.

"Ye-e-es," he said, without looking up.

"I was wondering if you could tell me anything about—"

"No."

"About the person who has been arrested this afternoon."

Now he looked up at me. His eyes were the color of the sea, alternately blue and gray. They were tiny and sharp, and his face screwed up around them as if he did not like what he saw. This was one Englishman who would be immune to my charms, I feared.

"There's nothing for you here, sir."

Oh, that "sir"! No one but an English country policeman could have invested it with so much sarcasm!

I thought I would take a chance. "I've been sent by Sir James Eagle to see—"

"Have you indeed." He shot a look at me with those distrustful little eyes that said, quite clearly, *You're lying.*

"—to check up on the young man's next of kin, see if anyone needs to be informed, that sort of thing."

"No, sir, there's no need for...'that sort of thing.' "

Now his rudeness was open. I saw little point in beating my head against a brick wall. Where were the guileless, malleable cops so useful to the heroes of detective literature?

I walked out of the station—and there he was. A copper so guileless, so malleable, that as soon as I saw his V-shaped torso swathed in blue serge and studded with silver buttons—not to mention the absurd helmet, just in the shape of a prick—I knew this was the man for Mitch Mitchell. He was waiting, oh so conveniently, right outside the station door, doing something entirely unnecessary to his bicycle wheel. As soon as I passed, he stood up—almost as if he were about to salute.

"Good afternoon," I said, taking note of a strong jawline and thick eyebrows that looked incongruous on a face that, in all other respects, bespoke innocence and trust. The moment I spoke, the young policeman broke into a grin.

"I know who you are," he said. "You're the American who's staying at the big house."

"Guilty as charged," I said, taking my time to scan up and down his uniform. He was a tidy piece of work; about 19 years old by the look of him.

"I...I like your accent, sir." I don't suppose he had heard the real McCoy before, except on the radio. Talking pictures had not yet arrived in Drekeham—but my little rookie was already half in love with America, and, I hoped, ready to go the rest of the way. He was exactly the sort of fresh-faced young man that I recognized as a particular English type: masculine, without being arrogant, and, though ignorant of vice, not averse to it.

"You do?" I said, with all the Bostonian twang I could muster. "Well, that's just...dandy." This had the desired effect, and he grinned even more broadly. "What's your name, officer?"

"PC Shipton, sir."

"Well, PC Shipton, I wonder if you'd be kind enough to show a visiting American around your station grounds. I'm...kinda interested in what you got back there."

If he thought this request was eccentric, he didn't show it. Perhaps an interest in the backs of police stations was exactly the sort of crazy whim that he expected from Yankees.

"Okay, pardner," he said, in the worst American accent I have ever heard. "This way."

He led me down an alley between the police station and the adjacent grocery store. It was wide enough for two men to pass at a pinch, and the broken cement of the floor was bursting with dandelions. I caught up with him and fell into step, our shoulders brushing. He was a good six inches taller than me, even without his helmet.

"This is where we wheel our bikes down," he said,

thankfully reverting to his own accent, which was broadest Norfolk, lilting up at the end of every sentence whether it was a question or not. "But I've got a puncture today, so I need to mend it."

"Hope your pump's working properly," I said, just to test the waters.

"Usually don't let me down, sir," he said, without a trace of double meaning. I glanced sideways at his eager face, the pale skin of his jawline just dusted with stubble.

"And here's the yard," he said, as we emerged into an untended garden that seemed to serve as a dumping ground for the station's unwanted furniture. There were filing cabinets at crazy angles, their drawers spilling open. There were old broken chairs, a couple of desks, and, in the longer grass, what looked unmistakably like the handle of a chamber pot. Nothing to excite suspicion: no obvious instruments of torture, no secret doorways, just the red brick back of the station that looked, to all intents and purposes, like an ordinary, dull family home.

"Gee, officer," I said, "that's neat."

He was tickled pink; listening to me speaking was obviously furnishing him with anecdotes for the pub.

"What else can I show you, sir?"

"What's that room there?" I pointed toward a window low in the back wall, covered with heavy-gauge wire mesh.

"That's the cell, sir."

"You just have one?"

"No, there's two. One there, for high-security prisoners, which we never use, this being Drekeham, and one just behind the front desk, where we put old Mr. Desmond if he's too drunk to get home on a Saturday night."

I could see a light gleaming through the dirty glass of the low window, and pointed this out to PC Shipton. He started, as if shocked.

"I think they must be cleaning it, that's all."

Had I strayed too far? I knew that I must not, at any cost, scare off my prize PC. I had to win his trust—or at least his obedience. I turned my back to the building, as if my interest was satisfied.

"And what's down there, at the end of the garden?" There was an outbuilding under a tree, and, beyond that, scrubby bushes.

"That's the bog—sorry, sir, the 'john,' where we go for a fag when we're not busy."

"I could do with a fag now, couldn't you?"

"Sure could, pardner!" He was off again, and I guessed that his alarm had passed. Fortunately for me, I had in my jacket pocket a pack of Lucky Strikes, which I kept about my person specifically for the impressing of young Brits. I myself smoked seldom, and only for effect. His eyes widened.

"Wow, look at that! Real American fags!"

"Care for one?"

"Better not. I'm on duty."

"I'd be mighty obliged..." Again, laying it on with a trowel did the trick.

"But if we went down the bog..."

"Exactly. Nobody can see you. Anyway, I expect everyone's very busy today. Too busy to care if you go off for a...fag."

"That's true enough," he said, not thinking what he was giving away. "Everyone's busy today indeed. Lot of blokes up from Norwich. Don't know what's—" He checked himself. "Anyway, down here's where we normally go for a quiet smoke, if we don't want to be interrupted."

"Down here" was a building quite unlike anything I had seen at home, nor indeed in Cambridge for that matter. I had been warned when I came to England that sanitation remained firmly in the nineteenth century, but I had yet to see anything quite so Victorian.

It was a building of crumbling red brick, about the size of the new war memorial in the village square, and just as ornate; obviously toilets of any sort were to be celebrated. You entered through a narrow, doorless opening that then doubled back on itself to shield occupants from prying eyes. Inside there were tiled walls that may once have been white, but were now so overgrown with algae and moss that the predominant color was green. There was a large urinal, where three men could have stood shoulder to shoulder, and a single cubicle, the door of which was pierced with a small square window, modestly covered with zinc mesh. The whole interior stank of piss and tobacco and sweaty men.

"So this is where you smoke," I said, redundantly; the floor was thick with cigarette butts.

"Yep," said Shipton, leaning against the wall and crooking one leg. He took off his helmet and placed it on the windowsill; I was delighted to see that, though so young, he was already starting to lose his hair. Premature baldness combined with heavy beard growth always seems to me to indicate a prodigious, unfussy sexual appetite. PC Shipton may not have been aware of this appetite yet. He was about to be made so. I tapped the bottom of the cigarette pack, and offered him a Lucky Strike. He took it between finger and thumb and put it to his lips, a gesture I always find delightful. And then he did something that, to me, is as erotically disturbing as many more obscene gestures; he undid the top button of his tunic, pulled it loose, and rubbed his throat. It made a scratching sound as he did so, though he had obviously shaved that morning.

I held a match to his face, and he bent forward, cupping his hands around the flame, then inhaled long and deep. The smoke came out in a long gray jet. Although I do not relish cigarette smoke, I love to see other men enjoying it. PC Shipton's appreciation of such a simple pleasure as a sneaky smoke promised well.

After I had feasted my eyes on this performance, I felt the need to take things a little further—and, fortunately for me, I had a full bladder to lend some credence to an admittedly hoary ploy.

"I need to take a leak," I said, stepping up to the urinal. I positioned myself near the middle, and proceeded to unbutton. PC Shipton saw nothing unusual in the act; we were, after all, in a lavatory. He did not offer to absent himself.

"Must be all that tea they make you drink up at Drekeham Hall, I bet," he said, laughing and puffing on his cigarette.

"Guess so."

"Reckon I need to go as well, now you mention it."

This was exactly what I had been hoping for. There is some primal instinct in the human male that drives us to communal pissing, and it's a phenomenon of which I'm very fond.

Due to my careful positioning, PC Shipton was obliged to stand close by me, whichever side he chose. He stationed himself to my right, fag in mouth, and began to fiddle with the front of his dark-blue uniform trousers. From the corner of my eye I could see his silver buttons shining, and a pale filament of smoke rising from his mouth.

I had pulled my dick out as far as possible—and, I'm glad to say, even in its resting state it's big enough to turn most men's heads. Given the location and the company, it had started to expand a little, and was looking more than usually plump. Before it got too hard, I closed my eyes, took a deep breath and cleared my mind; in order to make this look unplanned, I had better suit the action to the words. I'm not pee shy, and before long a thick yellow stream was splashing off the dirty white ceramic of the urinal. A few drops bounced back and, I noticed with delight, landed on PC Shipton's shiny boots.

By now the young copper had hauled his own truncheon

into view, and a handsome specimen it was: short, stubby, and, I immediately noticed, uncircumcised. The contrast had not passed him by either, and before he even started to piss, he said, with a chuckle, "Cor, look at that, sir! Roundheads and cavaliers!" I guessed he was not about to launch into a discussion of the English Civil War.

"You got something there that I don't."

"What, you mean this?" He tugged on his foreskin, stretching it out a good inch and a half. "We've all got this in my family."

"Looks good," I said, still pissing like a fire hose. He continued to play with his foreskin, now stretching it from side to side with the finger and thumb of each hand. I enjoyed the show, and my cock was starting to rise even further. Fortunately for me, I finished pissing before pissing became impossible. I did not put my cock away, but allowed it to hang out the front of my pants, where it stiffened and climbed in the cool, dank air.

"Anyway, better not play with it, might drop off," Shipton said, pulling his foreskin back a little way so that I could see a glimpse of peeping helmet. It looked shiny and slightly sticky compared to mine.

He turned his hips slightly toward me and started to urinate, completely unabashed. He enjoyed pissing, directing the stream up and down the wall of the urinal, describing circles and zigzags until he was done. Then he started shaking himself, a little harder than was strictly necessary. I stood with my hands on my hips, my cock by now unmistakably hard—and he could have no doubt, however innocent he was, that it was his performance that had made it that way. His own prick, which he seemed unwilling to relinquish, was already a good deal bigger than when I first saw it, and the foreskin, which had covered it so liberally before, was straining to contain the head.

We might have stood there modeling for each other had

not fate taken a kindly hand. PC Shipton, idly masturbating, exhaled a long jet of smoke—which went right into my eye. It hurt like hell. I winced and put my hands to my face in discomfort.

"Shit!"

"Oh, sir!" he said, quickly flicking his half-smoked cigarette into the gutter of the urinal, where it drowned in our mingled piss. "I'm so sorry! I'm always doing that!" His hands left his cock, and he placed them on my shoulders. "Try to open your eyes and blink, sir. That'll make it better."

I did as he told me, cursing the ease with which my eyes water when irritated. Tears were streaming down my face. He blew on my eyes, trying to soothe them; the tobacco on his breath wasn't pleasant, but the sensation was.

"Thank you, PC Shipton."

"It's Bill, sir."

"Thank you, Bill." For a moment the pain had made me forget that we were standing there airing our dicks. Then something reminded me: the tip of his, exposed by his now fully stretched foreskin, touched the tip of mine. His was going up, mine was going down, and they met halfway. He didn't remove his hands from my shoulders, but simply allowed our two cockheads to rest against each other. My move.

I always pride myself in recognizing the psychological moment, and acting on it. There was no longer any point in pretending that our communal pissing and dual erections were either coincidence or horseplay. This may have been new to PC Shipton (though I was beginning to wonder), but I knew full well that we had just crossed the Rubicon between "fooling around" and "having sex." I reached down with one hand and wrapped it around both our cocks, mashing them together so that they rolled and squashed against each other. I could feel just how hard he was—and, after a moment of doing this, I was fully as hard as him.

He still had his hands on my shoulders, and, when I looked up from the delightful spectacle of our fighting cocks, he was staring into my eyes.

"Sir... What are you doing?"

"I'm feeling your cock, Bill."

"Feels nice, doesn't it, sir?"

"Sure does. And this will feel nicer."

This was a bad day for my flannel trousers. They'd already gotten dusty in the cupboard, grassy and wet by the swimming hole, and covered in Boy Morgan's spunk. Now, as I knelt before my stiff young copper, they started soaking up a mixture of piss and cigarette ash. Mercifully, Drekeham Hall had an excellent laundry service.

With his cock at eye level, I had a chance to study it: I always like to take a good look at a cock I'm about to suck, and have never ceased to delight in the variety of shapes and sizes in which they come. This one was pale along the shaft, with a thick dorsal vein that branched an inch back from the head, which was the most beautiful, nacreous pink I have ever seen. I could wait no longer, and started to lick along the underside. This took my young copper by surprise.

"Jesus!" he shouted, clearly unaccustomed to the feel of tongue on cock, then hastily silenced himself and, for the next few moments, expressed his pleasure in heavy breathing and the occasional light moan. I licked every part of this cock, all along the sides, the top, around the ridge, and right into the piss slit, where I could still taste the sour, salty traces of his last release. My own cock was smearing what we used to call "pecker tracks" over his uniform trousers.

This tongue bath was sending young PC Bill into a kind of trance; when I looked up, his head was thrown back against the wall, his eyes half closed, his mouth half open, the strong column of his throat exposed. I had an urge to stand up and kiss him there—and yet there was another column demanding my attention, as a hefty throb from his now wet cock reminded me. The time had come to take him to the next stage—and if licking had rendered him so voluptuously abandoned, I wondered what sucking would do.

I engulfed his cockhead with my lips, then slid them down until he was touching the back of my throat. I guessed this was something that Norfolk girls didn't do.

"Fuck!" Bill barked. "Look at you!" I strained my eyes to look upward, and there he was, staring down, amazed by the sight of his prick stretching my mouth. Not breaking eye contact, I started to move up and down his stiffness; he was red in the face now, and completely in my power.

I had to remind myself at this point that I had not lured PC Shipton into the bog just to suck him off—not that I wouldn't have done so under normal circumstances, but in this instance I wanted something more from him. After sucking him for a while, I relinquished his cock and stood up. Masturbating him gently with one hand, I leaned the other palm against the wall beside his head. Our faces were only inches apart.

"How was that, copper?"

"I fucking loved it, sir. Please don't stop."

"Just one thing, Bill," I said, moving even closer, so that our lips were almost brushing.

"Yes, sir..."

"When we've finished, why don't you show me around the station?"

"Can't do that sir—oh, God!" I had squeezed his prick in such a way as to make him even stiffer.

"Please, Bill," I said. "For me." I didn't let him reply. With one swipe of my tongue, I opened up his lips and kissed him. This was all that was needed to reduce him to putty. He kissed me back with a passion I have seldom encountered in another man; I guess this was one young cop who was hungry for a bit of love.

We kissed rough and hard for a while, and then he broke off. Was this the moment at which he'd turn tail and run? I thought not.

"I've got to have you, sir," he said, as if the words were costing him dear. "I've got to feel you inside me."

I stepped back, my dick swinging and dripping with juice.

"It's all yours, Bill. Any way you want it."

He dropped to his knees and started smothering my cock in kisses; this wasn't going to be a particularly skillful blow job, I thought, but it would be sincerely meant. In between kisses, he would mutter some broken phrase like "Oh, God" or "I just...." I thought it best to let him get it out of his system. My cock was so hard now, and I was so excited by the sight of this overheated copper groveling before me, that I was close to coming. The sight of a small bald spot on the crown of his head pushed me toward the edge.

"Hold on, Bill," I said, "unless you want me to come in your face." From the look of devotion he gave me, I thought perhaps he wanted just that, but I had other ideas. "Let's find some privacy, shall we?"

I grasped his upper arm, brought him to his feet, and steered him toward the cubicle. It was spacious inside; really, were the municipal architects trying to facilitate sodomy?

Once inside, I lost no time in undoing Bill's trousers, and was delighted to find that his pale, round ass and stocky thighs were covered in dark-brown hair. I spat on a finger, slipped it inside him and saw his dick jump. Now he was sweating.

"Be careful, sir..."

"It's what you want, isn't it, Bill?"

"Yes sir. It's just..."

"It's okay, Bill. I won't hurt you."

"No sir."

Thank God for the obedience of the British working

class in those days. I did my utmost to be good to my word, working gobs of saliva into his hole until my fingers slid in and out quite easily. I pushed him forward so that he was bending over, his legs as far apart as his dropped trousers would allow them, his arms braced against the top of the toilet. My dick, which had been wet from his slobbering kisses, had dried now, but a handful of spit soon had it slick again, and I spread as much precum around the head as I could. I didn't want to hurt him—apart from anything else, I didn't want him shouting so much that he brought the entire North Norfolk Constabulary down upon us.

I nudged the head of my dick into position, and allowed him to get used to the feeling of penis against asshole. When he started shifting around as if to back onto me, I guessed he was ready for more. I slipped a hand around to caress his face: he immediately started licking and sucking my fingers. So, pulling his hips toward me, I made my entrance.

He didn't yell. There was a gasp, and a sharp intake of breath, of course. I didn't move. "Oh, my God, sir," he whimpered, "that hurts so much."

"Wait a bit, Bill," I said, knowing from plentiful experience on both sides of the act that the initial pain soon translates into pleasure. "I won't do anything."

I reached around to check the state of his cock; the first shock of entry had made his erection collapse. If this was going to be an enjoyable ride, he had better be as hard as possible. My fingers were still wet with spit, and I soon had him slicked up and standing at attention once again. His labored breathing turned to docile sighs, and I proceeded.

Now, when I pushed against him, the walls of his ass seemed to part in welcome, and in one glide I was up to the hilt.

"Are you inside me, sir?"

"Yes. All the way inside you." I held it still for a while, then squeezed my groin muscles so he'd feel me swell.

"You'd better fuck me then, because that's going to make me come in a minute."

He wasn't kidding. I started plowing into him, slowly at first, and from the tumult inside his ass it was evident that his orgasm was hurtling down the tracks at breakneck speed. Knowing that, at this stage, what you want more than anything is hard, fast, and even brutal treatment, I started throwing him a mighty fuck. My instincts were right. A steady, heavy flow of precum suddenly turned into something else, and my no-longer-virgin copper arched his spine and threw his head back. With a prolonged "Aaah..." he started squirting spunk into the toilet bowl as I jerked him off and fucked him simultaneously. The sight of his red face, the veins standing out in his throat, not to mention the tightening of his ass around my prick, had me grunting and spewing into his ass in no time. As I came, I did exactly what I had wanted to do since the moment I first saw him: I leaned forward and kissed him, long and hard, on the neck.

By the time we'd tidied ourselves up and emerged from the bog, the sun had practically set. PC Shipton wasn't the least bit gloomy, as I have known some young men to be after their first experience of dick; if anything, he had an extra spring in his step. His tunic was buttoned up high enough to cover the huge bruise I had left on his neck from kissing him—or cover most of it, anyway. Those with eyes to see would imagine that he had gotten carried away with some village sweetheart.

"Now, don't forget, Bill," I said, as we picked our way through the long grass and broken furniture of the station yard, "I want to see inside."

"Well that's against the rules, strictly speaking, sir."

"But you promised..."

He'd done nothing of the sort, of course, but what had just passed between us gave me sufficient leverage, should it come to that.

"If you were to go through that side door there," he said, pointing to a part of the building I had never noticed before, "you'd find yourself in the kitchen. After that I expect you'll find your way around."

"Won't you show me, Bill?"

He turned and looked at me with pleading eyes. "I would, sir," he said—and there was something in his voice that bespoke disquiet with recent events at Drekeham station. "But I daren't."

I fixed his gaze, to see if I could persuade him. Perhaps the suggestion of a quiet word with his superiors about goings-on in the station crapper?

There was nothing in his eyes but honest dismay. And there was little point in trying to get PC Shipton into trouble—any further than he already was, that is. Besides, I wanted to keep him sweet. He might be of further use, in any number of ways.

Shipton hurried back to the front of the building, leaving me loitering with obvious intent in the garden. I did not want to be seen; that mean desk sergeant would be only too glad to throw me out into the street, or into the cell more usually reserved for drunken Mr. Desmond. And so, keeping low, I hurried toward the side door that Bill had indicated. It opened with a gentle push, and I was in an old, barely used kitchen—not quite as unsanitary as the toilet, but far from spotless. I guessed that the local police took such refreshment as they needed at the homes and businesses of the local community.

Voices were audible from nearby, so I tiptoed over to the door and listened hard. They were close, and deliberately low. Did I dare go through that door, running the risk of falling straight into the clutches of Drekeham's finest? And, if not, was I prepared to throw away the advantage so hard won in the toilets?

Praying that the door didn't creak, I pulled it open—and,

to my unspeakable relief, it led to a dark, musty chamber, part pantry, part mess room. The voices I had heard were coming from the room beyond—and now that I was only separated by one partly open door, I could hear quite clearly. I crouched beneath the counter and listened.

What I heard removed any lingering doubt that what had been going on at Drekeham Hall that afternoon was villainy of the deepest dye.

IV

THERE WERE TWO VOICES. ONE I RECOGNIZED FROM Drekeham Hall: it was the man Sir James had addressed as "Sergeant," whose lack of surprise over the discovery of a dead body had so struck me. It was not a local voice; I was already accustomed to the Norfolk accent, had indeed just heard it burbling the most obscene endearments back in the toilets. The sergeant sounded to my ears closer to London. The other voice, however, was definitely local: gruff, low, the voice of an older man. Not the desk sergeant—he was obviously still elsewhere in the building, and I would have to watch my back.

"Right, Piggott," the sergeant said. "Your turn to see if you can get a confession out of him."

"I'll make him squeal, all right," Piggott, the older man, said, with a horribly salacious intonation. "He'll be crying like a fucking baby by the time I've finished with him."

"You can do whatever you want, as long as you don't kill him," the sergeant said.

"Bet you 'ave already, Sarge," Piggott said—and I swear I heard him licking his chops.

"I've prepared the way for you, yeah. Broken his spirit, as it were. Now it's up to you to finish the job off."

"You going to supervise, Sarge?"

"I think I'd better, don't you, Piggott? Make sure that proper police procedure is observed at all times."

"I'd do a better job that way, Sarge."

There was a burst of low laughter, then the sergeant shouted loud enough to be heard throughout the building, "Brown! Bring the prisoner to the interrogation room!"

There was a moment of silence, broken only by shifting and rustling from the other side of the door. I held my breath, desperate not to reveal my presence at this crucial moment. Then I heard the sergeant laughing again—though this time it was not such a cruel laugh.

"It hasn't got any smaller, then, Piggott."

This time it was Piggott's turn to laugh. "No, sir," he said, clacking his tongue in appreciation. "Still as big as the branch of a tree. Remember that, Sarge?"

"All too well, Piggott."

"And you bloody loved it, Sarge."

This was too much for my curiosity to stand. The door between the kitchen and the so-called interrogation room was one of those double-hinged affairs, with a round porthole window about seven inches in diameter in its upper half, to prevent collisions. I found that by seating myself on the counter but keeping no less than a foot away from the glass, I could see into the next room without allowing the light to shine on my face. There wasn't a great deal of light anyway: just one overhead lamp with a cheap tin shade that illuminated a small circular patch of floor. In this the policeman known as Piggott was standing, his trousers around his thighs, waving around a huge, semihard cock. The overhead lighting made it stand out as if it was glowing; the man's face was in deep shadow. From what I could see, he was short and thickset, dressed in a blue shirt, the tails of which hung down on either side of his dangling prick. His trousers, of course, were dark-blue, and his boots, where the light hit them, were highly polished. He was fair-haired and balding, and in the bright overhead light his head shone. His sleeves were rolled up, revealing strong plowman's forearms covered in a thick blond fleece. As for the sergeant, all I could make out was a darker moving patch against the general gloom; I dared not peer more closely for fear of discovery. But I remembered from the house that he was a smooth-faced, handsome young man with an arrogant, ironic bearing and cold, gray eyes. I thought at the time he was attractive; now that his cruel streak was being revealed, I was less certain.

The far door banged open.

"Get in there, you murdering little shit," came a voice I instantly recognized as the desk sergeant's. "Stand to attention when you're in the presence of your betters!" Then there was a thud, and an "Oof!," from beyond the scope of my vision.

"Bring the prisoner over here, Brown," the sergeant said. "Constable Piggott is going to interrogate him."

Piggott stepped out of the circle of light; all I could see of him now was one huge, hairy-knuckled hand working his prick to even more prodigious dimensions.

Much as I disapproved of what was going on, I happily could have watched the show for as long as it lasted—but my attention was drawn by something much more arresting. Meeks, the prisoner, had been thrust into the circle of light, where he instantly fell to his knees.

The last time I had seen Meeks, serving dinner at Drekeham Hall, I noted with approval his general neatness as well as the roundness of his bum. Now, things had changed. He had obviously received rough treatment in the cells; his shirt was torn and stained, his trousers filthy at the knees, and his face was bruised and dirty. There was a cut on his left cheekbone, not far from the eye, and the surrounding flesh was swelling and discolored. His lower lip was bulging, the neat beard matted with blood.

It struck me that Meeks did nothing to protest his condition, nor did he struggle. His expression remained as impassive as a Byzantine saint's. I could see clean tracks in the dirt on his cheeks that showed he had been weeping in the privacy of his cell; now, however, his eyes were dry and downcast.

"Decided to talk yet, have we?" Piggott said, positioning himself behind the kneeling prisoner and waving his prick at him like a schoolyard bully.

Meeks remained silent, head bowed, hands resting on his thighs.

"Come on, you little bastard, we know you did it. Just say the word and you can go."

Meeks shook his head—a tiny movement, but enough to enrage his interrogator.

"Don't you fucking deny it, you piece of scum," Piggott shouted, working himself into a fury. I knew from the football field and the boxing ring back home that this kind of channeled aggression was necessary in order to pull off feats of daring. In Piggott's case, cruelty made his cock bigger and harder. He started swinging his hips, smacking his prick against the side of Meeks's cropped brown head. "Fucking confess, you bastard, or I'll have you."

Meeks did nothing. With one hand, Piggott pressed the length of his cock against Meeks's neck, exposed now that the collar had been torn off, and started thrusting his hips so the whole thing slid up and down against his throat. The head, exposed with every thrust, was a huge, bulbous thing, deeply grooved around the piss slit.

"Make him suck it," came the sergeant's voice from beyond the ring of light.

"He'll suck it, all right," Piggott said, grabbing Meeks's ear and yanking his head into an uncomfortable twist, which brought the uncontrollably thrusting prick into contact with his lips. "If he won't say the words we want him to say, we'll just have to put something else into his mouth, won't we."

Even now, with a huge, brutal cock sliding all over his face, Meeks's expression betrayed nothing. This infuriated Piggott even more. He reached down and forced the prisoner's jaws apart with one huge hand, then, stretching Meeks's lips wide open, jammed in as much of his cock as would fit. When he removed his fingers, his cock was planted firmly inside Meeks's mouth. With one hand holding Meeks's chin, Piggott began to fuck his face—without much finesse, I thought. Tears ran down Meeks's cheeks as he gagged, trying not to choke on Piggott's thrusting prick.

"See if he's ready to confess now, Piggott." Piggott pushed Meeks off his cock, and he fell back on his heels, his head hanging low.

"Come on, Meeks, all you have to do is tell us that you killed him. That's all we want to hear."

Silence.

"You're not helping anyone. Least of all yourself. If you don't confess, we'll just keep on doing what we're doing until..."

My mind was working rapidly. It was quite clear that Meeks was innocent, a convenient fall guy for a crime that even I, with my rudimentary powers of deduction, could see was fishy. I didn't think that they would kill him in police custody—that would lead to far too many awkward questions—but I wondered how much more of this treatment Meeks could take before confessing to a crime he did not commit.

And so I decided to do something very foolish.

Jumping off the kitchen counter, I blundered through the swing door and into the interrogation room.

"Who the fuck..."

"Shipton, I told you to stay out of here."

They could hear me, but not see me—so Piggott grabbed the light and shined it full in my eyes.

"Excuse me, officers"—again, my best dumb Yank accent. "I appear to be lost."

Piggott let go of the lamp as if it was burning him, and rapidly stuffed his still-wet cock back into his pants. The light swung wildly about the room, our shadows dancing before and behind us with sickening speed.

"How did you get in here?" The sergeant's voice was icy.

"I was just looking around your garden and I guess I got lost."

"What did you see?"

"Well, I guess the grass could do with cutting..." Meeks was looking up at me, beseeching me with his eyes. "Oh, hello, Meeks," I said, as if I'd only just seen him. "I heard that they'd brought you here. I hope everything is okay."

Piggott pulled the prisoner to his feet—somewhat less roughly than he'd handled him before, I was glad to note—and bundled him out of the room. As they left, I said, "Don't worry, Meeks. I'll be down again in the morning with your lawyer."

The sergeant was still in the room, prowling around the outer darkness, occasionally illuminated by the swinging lamp, presumably thinking how best to deal with this unwanted witness.

"You'd better leave," he said, stepping up and eyeballing me. His eyes were disconcerting: the palest, iciest gray I have ever seen, with a strange, distant look, as if he was focusing on a point behind my head.

"Certainly, officer. I'm sorry to have intruded." *But not half as sorry as you are to have a witness of just how the English police treat their prisoners*, I thought. "I'll find my own way out."

I did not want to overplay an already weak hand, so, as the sergeant began to advance toward me, I turned and fled. The early-evening light in the overgrown garden was blinding, and I stumbled over a broken chair frame as I made my way back to the front of the building and walked briskly up the road.

As I reached the village green, I saw Shipton walking his bike back toward the station. He looked forlorn.

"What ho, Bobby!" I said, in a terrible imitation of an English accent. "Why the long face?"

"I've got a hole in my back tire, sir."

"Not as nice as the hole in your backside, Bill."

He blushed and grinned sheepishly. "Oh, well, about that, sir..."

There was nobody around, so, feeling reckless, I stretched up and planted a kiss on his open mouth.

"Oh, sir! Anyone might have seen!"

I grabbed his crotch; something was already stirring. He'd keep.

"Take care of this for me, Bill," I said. "Never know when I might need it." And, with my hands in my pockets, I strolled off, whistling a merry tune. After all, it's always handy to have a friend in the police force.

V

DINNER THAT NIGHT WAS A STRAINED AFFAIR. SIR JAMES was taciturn and brooding—and when a man of his considerable personality decides to brood, everybody knows it. I compared him—not favorably—to my own father, who, even in his darker moments, could always be brought around with a joke or a dig in the ribs. But when Sir James Eagle retreated to the lofty heights of his ego, nobody, not even his wife, dared disturb him.

Lady Caroline was gracious and placid at dinner—she was always gracious and placid. I suspect she maintained those qualities throughout the war, and would remain so even if a bomb were to go off under her chair. A bomb was, indeed, ticking in Drekeham Hall, though at the time I did not know the scale of the coming explosion.

Leonard Eagle, Sir James's younger brother whom I had got to know so well in the secret swimming pool earlier that afternoon, kept the conversation going with aplomb, chattering on about this or that friend of the family, relaying the latest gossip from the London circuit, with which he seemed extremely familiar (though rumor had it that he was no longer welcome in some Mayfair houses). I didn't like the man, whatever skills he possessed, but I was grateful to him for keeping silence at bay. I was less grateful for the occasional forays that his elegantly shod foot made under the table, up my shin, and into my groin—not least because I was also under attack from my right, where Boy Morgan was "accidentally" allowing his hand to rest on my thigh.

For this I had only myself to blame; while dressing for dinner in our shared bedroom, I spent as long as possible completely naked, padding around without a stitch just inches away from him. Morgan lay on the bed in a toweling robe, which every so often fell open to reveal his obvious interest in further relations. I feigned not to notice. For one thing, I was somewhat tired, having already had more sex in one day than, strictly speaking, I needed. Furthermore, I was saving myself for the night; I intended, by bedtime, to have worked Morgan into such a state that neither of us would get much sleep. And so, as we sat through soup and fish and meat and dessert and cheese, Morgan found a hundred reasons to touch me, his hand creeping a little nearer my crotch each time. I feared that, unless I was careful, Leonard's foot would meet Morgan's hand, and the game would be up. It's nice to be wanted, but not always convenient.

The rest of the party was equally glum. Poor Belinda, who sat on Morgan's right, was snappish and sulky, perhaps because of the shock she had received that afternoon—I suppose that, even in aristocratic English families, young ladies aren't trained to behave well on discovery of a corpse—but also because her dashing fiancé was almost completely ignoring her. This was hardly surprising. Morgan's attempts to "comfort" her, when I left them together earlier in the afternoon, met with a peevish rebuff, as he'd told me before dinner. I sympathized, talking a lot of airy nonsense about women (as if I had any experience in that field!) while noting with delight that Morgan was getting as frustrated as any twenty-year-old man could be. The social strictures of the 1920s, which forbade heterosexual relations outside marriage, were very much on my side.

We were six at the table. Next to Leonard, opposite Belinda, was the glacially unfriendly Lady Diana "Whopper" Hunt, who had arrived hotfoot from Trouville that very afternoon. She treated everyone and everything—guests, staff, food, drink—with distaste. She always looked as if someone nearby had just farted—exactly that look of disgust on her downturned mouth. Perhaps, I thought, trying to be charitable, she was missing her own fiancé, Rex Eagle, whose sudden absence on "London business" had still not been adequately explained. But she didn't look like the type who would pine over anyone's absence. Rex, from the little I knew him, was a serious but decent young man, still a rowing legend at Cambridge, whence he had graduated two years previously. He was jolly and friendly when he wanted to be, and had made me feel quite welcome at Drekeham Hall—but there was something guarded about him. Perhaps that was the fate of the older son. Serious Rex may have been—but even he could surely not have been attracted to Diana Hunt's frigid hauteur. I sensed dynastic reasons for the marriage; it certainly wasn't a love match.

We reached dessert in safety. Leonard was prattling on about some wild party he'd been to at the public baths, "which they'd turned into a Palm Court for the occasion, with a Negro orchestra, and they served the most delightful bathwater cocktails, mostly gin I suspect, very drunk-making, everyone had a very gay time" (at which he rolled his eyes and ground his foot into my balls). Everyone else stared into their rhubarb crumble, desperately trying to think of something to say. He carried on throughout the cheese course, treating us to a hair-raising account of a recent "jape" around the East End. (I suspect it was highly censored.) When the ladies withdrew, and we men were left to discuss the weighty matters of the day, Sir James lit a fat cigar and lost himself in wreaths of smoke. Leonard brought from his breast pocket a stylish silver cigarette case, from which we younger men helped ourselves. The staff cleared the plates, port was passed. (I can't stand the stuff, and took only a thimbleful before passing it to Morgan, who guzzled.)

Once the coast was clear, Leonard strayed onto dangerous ground.

"Well, gentlemen, what a ghastly day."

The remark was greeted with silence, and I assumed Leonard would be tactful enough to retreat to safer subjects, like politics or religion.

"Imagine, the police in Drekeham Hall."

Sir James scowled at his brother, but did not venture an opinion.

"And to think of that poor dead young man, lying on a slab somewhere..."

"That's enough, Leonard," Sir James said, in the voice that had regularly quelled the House of Commons.

"Well, I can't help feeling sorry for him, and his family, if it comes to that," continued Leonard, who, having ignored his brother all his life, wasn't about to start paying attention to him now. His eyes were fixed on me throughout.

"But really, what can you expect when people bring the lower orders into the house?"

Sir James sighed, and put his head in his hands—but, to my surprise, said nothing.

"At least the police have their man," Leonard continued.

This was clearly for my benefit; I wondered if words had passed between Drekeham Police Station and the big house after my earlier visit.

"But surely you don't think Meeks killed him?" I asked, playing the role expected of me.

"Oh, but there's no doubt of it, I'm afraid. The man's...well, how shall I put this? Mentally unstable."

"Absolute rot. I've never seen a more stable person in my life." *A good deal more stable than you, Leonard Eagle*, I thought.

"Appearances can be so deceptive, Mr. Mitchell," Leonard said, narrowing his eyes. "Are any of us truly what we appear to be? Take your friend Mr. Morgan, for instance..."

Morgan, too far gone on port to pay much attention, looked up, red in the face, and grunted when he heard his name mentioned.

"Now, to look at him, you'd think Harry Morgan was nothing more than a Cambridge hearty, useful on the rowing team and a decent shot, perhaps. Who would dream that he was such a...sensitive and intelligent young man?"

Insinuations? Or something more? What had Leonard seen? In some sense, I was being warned.

"But Meeks, of all people. Surely, Sir James, you know the man well enough to realize..."

Leonard interrupted. "I'm sorry to say we've expected something of the sort from Meeks for a while now. I urged James to send him packing, but no—he wouldn't hear of it, he has this admirable sense of loyalty to his staff. And now look what's happened."

"And what has happened, may one ask?"

"Oh, for God's sake..." Sir James said, turning away from the table. Why did he not silence his brother? Why did he not suggest we "join the ladies," a surefire way of bringing to a close any awkward conversation. Instead he stayed silent and suffering while Leonard carried on.

"The poor, unfortunate young man, Mr.... What was his name, Jim?"

"Walworth," Sir James said with a sigh. "Reg Walworth."

"Of course, Reginald Walworth. The poor, unfortunate Mr. Walworth came to Drekeham Hall as Meeks's guest. A delightfully democratic idea in theory, Jim, but one that can only lead to anarchy and tragedy, as has been demonstrated. My brother has always treated his staff as equals. Perhaps now he has learned his lesson."

"So, if Walworth was a friend of Meeks," I asked, "why would he kill him?"

"Oh, Mr. Mitchell, you have a lot to learn about life belowstairs in an English country house. Suffice to say that Meeks had somewhat...how can I put this in words that Mr. Morgan will understand? Somewhat vicious tastes. The unfortunate Mr. Walworth was the latest in a string of young men of frankly criminal physiognomy whom Meeks had entertained at Drekeham Hall. It's a miracle that we've avoided a scandal for so long. And now, I fear, Meeks's inclinations got the better of him. He went too far. Too far. How dangerous it is when we overstep the mark."

"What will happen to him?"

"He will be tried for murder in Norwich and he will doubtless hang for it."

"That's unspeakable. The man is innocent."

"You seem very sure, Mr. Mitchell. Upon what do you base your conviction?"

I was not about to say what I had seen in the police station; better to keep my powder dry for when I really needed it. And so I fudged. "I reckon I'm a pretty good judge of human nature..."

"Without disrespect to you, Mr. Mitchell, I believe that your experience of the world may be somewhat...limited. I am sure that, in America, your straightforward view is entirely justified. Good is good, bad is bad, that sort of thing. Over here, however, you'll find that there are so many intermediate stages. So many different things to be considered. So many...conflicts of interest."

In other words, don't poke your nose in where it's not wanted. Leonard had said what he had to say, and, pushing back his chair, suggested that we join the ladies. I had to rouse a sleepy Morgan with a nudge, and hoped that there would be sufficient strong coffee in the drawing room to wake him up for bedtime.

Leonard had let me know that my actions had not gone unnoticed; time for me to let him know that I was aware of wrongdoing in Drekeham Hall. As Sir James opened the doors to the drawing room, engaged in some comforting conversation with Morgan about recent sporting events, I took Leonard by the elbow and steered him to a quiet spot under the sweeping staircase, where we would not be observed.

"Why, Mr. Mitchell, so urgent!" He must have thought that his tickling throughout dinner had inflamed me. It had, but for once the investigative organ overruled the generative.

"I know I'm only a guest in this house, Lennie," I said, stressing the familiarity, "but I will not be party to a crime."

"Good Lord," he said, grabbing my crotch none too gently, "it's a bit late to start worrying about that, isn't it, Mitch?"

"That's not what I'm talking about." He had a point; what we had done, and what I intended to do to Morgan in an hour or two, was very much against the law.

"Tell that to the magistrates, Mr. Mitchell," he said, rubbing and squeezing me until I began to respond. Of course he thought I could be thrown off the scent by a bit of judicious cockplay; that much he had discovered before, when he so conveniently got me out of the house.

I had no choice but to bluff my way to higher ground. "I think the tastes of a foreigner like me would be of very little interest compared to what goes on in the private life of an MP and his family."

Bull's-eye. Leonard relinquished his grip on my crotch and looked me spitefully in the eye.

"You know nothing of what goes on in this house."

"I know enough to put every single one of you on the front page of the newspapers." This was a lie, but evidently it contained a germ of truth. How far did the corruption of the Eagle household go?

"And what would that achieve, Mr. Mitchell," Leonard said, suddenly changing his tone to one of friendly worldliness. "Another fine family dismantled, a great career destroyed—my brother's, I mean, not mine. I don't have one—and a great deal of unpleasant talk about people like you and me. No fun for anyone."

He had a point, but I had an advantage, and I wasn't going to surrender it.

"Some things are more important than fun. The hanging of an innocent man, for instance."

"Mr. Meeks, my dear fellow, is far from innocent."

"Bullshit."

"Spare me your home-on-the-range vulgarities, Mr. Mitchell. Mr. Meeks is as guilty as any of us, if you must expose guilt. What goes on in this house is one big guilty secret. Has been for years. Oh, everyone thinks I'm the debauched, disgusting one, but let me tell you, the reason why I had to get out, to start a new life for myself in London, is precisely because I was disgusted by what goes on in Drekeham Hall. Just because something has happened for a very long time doesn't make it good. James turns a blind eye because it's 'tradition,' and he has a great respect for tradition, but he's wrong."

"What are you talking about?"

"Oh, come on. You know the game. It's like a great big daisy chain. The butler buggers the first footman, the first footman buggers the second footman, who buggers the hall boy, who buggers the boots; the head gardener buggers the under gardener, who buggers the nurseryman, who buggers the stable boy. Shall I go on? Have you never wondered why there are so few female staff at Drekeham Hall? Just that gorgon of a housekeeper, Mrs. Ramage, a couple of chambermaids, and kitchen maids. The whole place is Sodom-by-the-Sea."

"Oh, don't be—"

"And Mr. Meeks, not content with having all that delightful trade on his plate, must needs import it from outside. He went on these little...what shall we call them? Expeditions, perhaps, to Norwich at first, then to London, bringing back young men and introducing them to the household as 'hired hands.' Well it wasn't their hands that were hired, that much I can tell you. The things that go on belowstairs in this house... And let us just say that this afternoon, while the rest of us were engaged in the wholesome and delightful game of Sardines, there were sports going on elsewhere of a far more dangerous nature."

"I don't believe a word of it."

Leonard ignored me. "And I'm afraid that the unfortunate Mr. Reg Walworth lost the game."

"What exactly happened to him?"

"I have no desire to find out. The police said he had been asphyxiated. I can only imagine how. Behind that servile facade, Mr. Meeks is, I believe, a somewhat vigorous lover."

I was speechless. There seemed no doubting the truth of Leonard's revelations.

"So now you must leave us to sort things out in our own way," he continued, sensing my defeat. "With Meeks out of the way, we can take back some control of the staff. The rest of them, with one or two exceptions, are a reasonable bunch. The butler is a dear. The chef isn't bad, for a foreigner. Even the hall boy, what's his name, Simon, is a sweetie, though the poor soul is deaf and doesn't know what's going on half the time. I'm sure he could tell a few tales. People think he's stupid, but he's not. You should have a chat with him. I'm sure you'd find him very eager to oblige."

Leonard had overplayed his hand; I knew instantly I was being fobbed off with a pat on the head and a sweetie for being a good boy. Presumably Leonard reasoned that if I was busy fucking the oh-so-accommodating hall boy, I would drop my amateur investigation of the Mystery of the Throttled Trade. And it was probably better that he should think that.

"Oh, yes," I said, "I've noticed him. Very nice looking kid." He was, too, with his sleepy eyes and silky skin, his air of uncomplaining servility. I'd noticed him the moment I walked into Drekeham Hall.

"Very nice indeed," Leonard said, resuming his expert stroking of my prick. I now allowed myself to grow hard, which wasn't difficult, as his ministrations hit all the right spots.

"And now," he said, "I shall go and join the ladies, who, thank God, know nothing of all this."

"I'll come with you."

"Oh, Mr. Mitchell," Leonard said, acting like an abashed debutante, "I think you'd better wait a minute or two. The poor dear ladies would faint if you took that"—giving my cock a last squeeze—"into the drawing room."

With that, he darted out from under the stairs and, wiggling his backside in farewell, scuttled off to join the rest of the party.

Tempted as I was to pour my frustrations into the mouth of Simon, the hall boy, I could not ignore certain inconsistencies in Leonard Eagle's generally brilliant attempt to put me off the scent. First of all, if Meeks was so hardened in vice, why had he gone so uncomplainingly to his incarceration in Drekeham Police Station? His martyrlike manner under Piggott's unorthodox "interrogation" was not the behavior of a man used to bullying and corruption. Nor was he playing along with the police, enjoying the ride, as might have been expected from what Leonard had told me. His attitude, as far as I had seen, was one of patient resignation—the resignation of a man who knows he is innocent, but is powerless to prove it.

Second, and more bothersome, Leonard's tales of belowstairs buggery did not explain Sir James's gloomy *froideur* at dinner. Certainly, it was a blow to his democratic ideals to find that his laissez-faire management methods had resulted in a death—but if this was the case, surely he would have been down there busting heads rather than wreathing himself in smoke through a family dinner. Even taking into account that there were guests in the house, inconvenient witnesses in the form of Morgan and myself, I would have expected a man of action like Sir James to act, not to ponder. Something was holding him back. I could see that he was chafing under the insinuations of his younger brother, and yet he kept quiet. This was inconsistent with the facts as they had been presented to me.

Also—and for this I kicked myself—there was something odd about the way in which the body had been discovered and disposed of. Belinda had found it in a cupboard—almost certainly not the scene of the crime—and was under the impression that it had been dragged there from Sir James's dressing room. At the time I was quick to dismiss this as the muddled memory of a nice, but not bright, girl. I'm ashamed to say that I didn't like Belinda much; the truth was that I was jealous of the affection Boy lavished on her, even if it was I who was getting his cock. I had her down as an empty-headed flapper—and I was wrong. I began to wonder if, after all, her observations had been correct, and the body had come not from belowstairs—not directly, at any rate—but from somewhere much more incriminating. Little wonder, if that was true, that Leonard was so eager to distract me with Simon, the hall boy's, beautiful backside.

With these thoughts occupying my brain, I was very quickly in a fit state to present myself to the ladies; nothing like deductive reasoning to take the blood out of a stiff prick. I did my best to chat and charm, figuring that I would need friends throughout the house if I was going to get to the truth of things. I discussed politics with Lady Diana, I chattered about interior design with Lady Caroline, who wanted to have the drawing room "done over" by Syrie Maugham, all in white, and I attempted to tell Sir James a little of political and economic life in Boston. I flatter myself that I handled all subjects with aplomb, but my mind was elsewhere, worrying at the problem of Meeks and the murdered man like a dog around a bone.

As the clock struck eleven, and Morgan was yawning and dozing in his chair, Burroughs, the butler, arrived to clear away the cups and glasses and to take any orders for the following day. He was a charming old fellow, straight out of a novel: short, slightly stooped, frail and white-haired, sporting a little pair of steel-rimmed spectacles that added the final touch to his butler's mien. I thought him delightful when I first saw him, so perfectly did he incarnate my American ideas of English servanthood; I think, also, he thought me delightful, as his gaze had more than once lingered about my person with a certain fondness. He was discretion itself, however, and never attempted to engage me in conversation on any topic other than my needs as a guest.

Now, however, he seemed eager to talk—despite the watchful eyes of Leonard and Sir James.

"Are you and Mr. Morgan quite comfortable in your room, sir?" he asked in hushed tones, as he placed my glass on a silver tray.

"Perfectly, thanks, Burroughs."

"If there's anything you need, please don't hesitate to ring."

"Thank you."

"I will attend you in person."

"Righto."

He lowered his voice to a whisper. "So if you have any questions at all, sir, about the running of the house..." Our eyes met; his were quite red, as if he'd been crying. "Do please just let me know."

He was risking much by talking to me in this way, and I had no desire to worsen his situation. "Thank you, Burroughs," I said, loud enough for all to hear, "a seven o'clock call would be just fine, and kippers for me. What about you, Boy? Kippers okay?"

"Yuck," Morgan said, stretching his long arms. "Bacon and eggs for me, anytime."

"One kipper, one bacon," Burroughs said, with a grateful smile. "Will there be anything else, Sir James?"

"No thanks, Burroughs. We've all had a very tiring day. Best if you get some sleep. Tomorrow...well, tomorrow will be hard."

Lady Caroline leaned over to Sir James and squeezed his hand. He neither looked up, nor smiled, nor returned the pressure. He was a man utterly alone with this thoughts.

After the dreadful day and miserable evening I had spent, I needed some recompense before I went to sleep—and, as I have often found before exams, the best way to come afresh to a problem is to take one's mind off it completely for a few hours. And I have never found anything that takes my mind off things as effectively as the pursuit of sex with other men.

Morgan was my quarry, of course; his conquest was the reason why I had accepted the invitation to Drekeham Hall in the first place, figuring that the strange surroundings and our enforced proximity would lead to the long-desired outcome. We'd already done the foreplay, in the cupboard and in the bathroom, where he had come down my throat. But this was nothing compared to what I had planned—and, murder or no murder, tonight was the night he was going to get what was coming to him.

Morgan had been half-asleep for the last hour before bedtime, bored to death by the conversation, warmed by the wine and port and exhausted by a trying day. Sir James and Lady Caroline would occasionally look over to see him nodding off in his chair, while poor, neglected Belinda tinkled aimlessly on the piano or tried to engage Lady Diana in girlish small talk, for which she showed no inclination. The prospective parents-in-law didn't think much of Boy Morgan's intellectual abilities, that was clear, but it was impossible to dislike him. Dull at times he may have been, but I have never found a truer heart.

When we rose to retire and said our good-nights, Morgan perked up, and took the stairs two at a time, as I had seen him do so often at Cambridge. "Christ, that was a boring bloody evening," he said. "I wish we could have gone to the pub."

"Fear not, Boy. The night is young."

He almost ran along the landing to our room; I was in hot pursuit.

"I say, I hope you don't think this is absolutely dreadful, but I've borrowed a bottle of whisky from Old Man Eagle's cellar. Burroughs brought it up earlier. Sound man, Burroughs."

"Sound indeed." How useful: another pretext for Morgan to "lose control" of himself. The bottle was neatly tucked inside a pitcher that stood on the dressing table; Morgan poured shots into two tooth glasses and handed me one.

"Here's how," he said, knocking his back and replenishing it instantly. I feigned a swig, but took only a sip. He didn't notice; he was concerned only with achieving a desirable degree of intoxication. What it is to have inhibitions, I thought; little wonder there are so many ruined livers.

"Can't wait to get out of this bloody suit of armor," he

said, undoing his bow tie with a smart tug and fiddling with his collar studs. "Fellow can't breathe with all this on."

This sounded like an invitation to me, so I stepped up to face him.

"Here. Let me. It's easier." Morgan's hands fell down by his sides as I undid the studs at the back and front of his collar and dropped them neatly on the dressing table.

"That's better," he said. "Hot as hell in that drawing room."

"Better make you comfortable, then." I slipped his dinner jacket off his shoulders, and allowed it to fall straight from his arms into a heap at his feet.

"Mitch..."

"Yes, Boy?"

"What we're doing..."

"Mmm?"

"It's not... I mean you don't think..."

"Don't worry. Just enjoy yourself."

"But I mean, I'm not..."

"'Course you're not. I understand that."

"Thing is, though..."

He was silent for a while; his hair, which had been unattractively slicked back all evening, now fell dark and oily over his brow.

"What?"

"Oh, dash it," he said, with wonderfully impetuous sportiness—and kissed me full on the mouth. One hand held the back of my neck as his tongue parted my lips; the other squeezed the muscles of my upper arm. I guess that whatever argument Boy had been having with himself had been resolved in my favor.

Thus far in our "courtship," I had been the hunter, Morgan the game. Now, to my surprise and delight, the tables were turned. Not content with kissing me as if his life depended on it, Morgan tore off my jacket, which joined his on the floor, and started unbuttoning my shirt. He wasn't terribly proficient with buttons and studs, but I found his hurried fumbling much more exciting than any slicker performance would have been. I managed to get out of collar and tie, and my shirt fell open to the waist. I'm naturally hairy on my torso, and have been since my mid-teens—and Morgan, whose chest was smooth apart from a small growth of hair in the valley of his chest, dived straight in with his tongue. He rubbed his face and mouth against my chest like a cat making up to its owner.

I pulled his shirttails out of his trousers, then drew the entire garment over his head, exposing the bumps and curves of a long, elegant spine surrounded by the muscles of a champion rower. They rippled as Morgan moved his arms to free himself for further exploration of my torso; by now he had worked his way down to my stomach and was bent at a right angle from the waist. With him in this position I could only think of one thing—fucking his virgin ass—but I decided to let him maintain control for the time being. He seemed so hell-bent on what he was doing that it would have been unkind to stop him.

After making love to my navel for a minute, he broke for air and stood up, allowing me a full view of his beautiful, athletic physique. His face and neck were flushed, partly from the whisky, partly from contact with my body hair, which was wiry in places. Saliva glistened around his mouth, spread by the wet whorls of hair on my chest and stomach. The front of his trousers were stretched by a very obvious hard-on.

"Please strip for me, Mitch. I want to see you."

I obliged, and, even with braces and buttons to negotiate, was naked within a minute. I was every bit as hard as Morgan, my prick standing out from a thick bush of hair, a drop of stickiness just appearing at the slit. Morgan stared at it as if hypnotized, preparing himself to take what, for him, was a very large step indeed—the step that would turn him from a jolly good chap and a Cambridge rower into a cocksucker.

He took the step.

In a flash he was on his knees, smothering my cock with kisses, determined, it seemed, to leave no part of it unloved. He started licking it, pulling gently on my balls, doing the things to me that he had done to himself—and enjoyed—in private. He already knew how good another mouth can feel down there, so, closing his eyes and taking a deep breath, he opened wide and closed his lips around my cockhead. When he looked up at me, his big trusting eyes full of questions, I almost shot my load right there. Had I not already had such a tiring day, I might well have done so.

I caressed his head, playing with his thick black hair, gently drawing him further down onto me. I did not expect him to become an instant expert at a practice that it had taken me many months to perfect, but he made a pretty good attempt for a beginner, running his lips down to the halfway mark, but pulling back when he felt my prick entering the back of his mouth. I had no desire to put him off cocksucking by making him gag on his first attempt, so I contented myself with only half fucking his mouth. Practice would make perfect.

I noticed that, while eating my dick, Morgan had released his own cock from his pants and was slowly masturbating himself. This was too much to resist, so, pulling out of his mouth, I knelt in front of him and took him in my hands. We kissed again, and I pulled him to the floor and straight into the 69 position. I was totally naked; he was shirtless, but still in his trousers and shoes, his cock sticking out of the fly.

There was a real danger that we were going to come too soon; I didn't want Morgan to find release before I had broken him in more fully. I stopped sucking him and rolled him onto his back. He was reluctant to relinquish my cock, but in this position had little choice but to allow me to undress him, pulling off one shoe, one sock, another shoe, another sock.... He extended his legs and lifted his ass to allow me to draw off his trousers, then his underpants, and finally I had him naked before me. I think he had a good idea of what was coming next.

"I say, Mitch, I'm not sure..."

I had an infallible trick for allaying the fears of any young man about to discover his anus for the first time. Diving down between his parted cheeks, I began to lick his hole, probing my tongue in gently but firmly. This usually comes as a shock, but the pleasure that follows immediately in its wake is a persuasive argument. Morgan, whose fears in this area seemed very slight, was soon moaning and lifting his hips from the carpet.

His ass was as beautiful as the rest of him, pink and clean and juicy, as sweet as a plum. I ate it until I judged that he was as relaxed and aroused as he could be. Then I pulled back and looked him in the eyes.

"I want to fuck you, Morgan," I said.

"Oh..."

"Do you want me to?"

He couldn't actually frame the word *Yes*, but I understood that the long "Mmmmm" and the further opening of his legs were answer enough.

There was no point in delaying; I didn't want his willingness, or his hard-on, to subside. So I reached up to the dressing table, found the pot of brilliantine with which Morgan had dressed his hair before dinner, took a large blob on the end of two fingers, and worked it liberally around his hole. It opened up and practically swallowed my hand.

Smearing another blob of cream onto my prick, I lined it up with the target, applied the slightest of forward pressure, and waited. At first there was resistance; Morgan had seen for himself how big my cock is and perhaps feared that, if half its length had nearly made him gag, the whole thing could do mischief to his insides. But then the heat of flesh against flesh worked its old magic, and his asshole opened up and engulfed me.

Once the head was in, I wanted to pile-drive into him, but proceeded with caution; I've had lovers myself who rushed this crucial stage of the journey and ruined the rest of the ride. So I allowed him to get used to feeling something inside him, and rested there, tossing him gently. He had softened slightly when I entered him; I wanted him to be hard before I continued. This didn't take long.

"Oh, God," he said, as new sensations came thick and fast, "this is incredible."

"Just wait," I said, inching forward. He held his breath, but remained as stiff as a post. I judged it safe to proceed, and slowly pressed ahead until I was up to the hilt in his anus. Morgan's face registered amazement, and he was sweating—but not for nothing had he spent all those hours training to withstand physical exertion. His stomach muscles rippled, he breathed deeply and regularly, and I felt his ass tightening and loosening around me.

"Okay, Mitch," he said, with a businesslike tone that almost made me laugh, "you can fuck me now."

And I did. I fucked him rotten. I fucked him on his back, with his legs over my shoulders, staring down into his eyes. I turned him over and pulled him onto all fours, and fucked him from behind, pounding into him as hard as I have into anyone. I fucked him on his side, one leg held in the air as his cock drizzled the carpet with juice. Finally I dragged him to the bed, lay him down, placed a couple of cushions under his ass and began the long ride to my goal.

I wanted him to come first; I wanted him to know the incomparable feeling of coming while a man is fucking you, of feeling him inside you after you've come, when you think you can no longer stand the sensation but don't want it to stop. This was easily managed. After that initial brief softening, Morgan remained as solid as a rock throughout the fuck. Occasionally he tugged on his cock, but stopped short of anything decisive. Now, however, I grabbed his wrist, placed his hand on his dick and moved it up and down a few times. I like to see a man masturbate himself while I fuck him; I like to imagine that he is feeling what I am feeling.

Morgan was quick on the uptake, and picked up the pace of his wanking to match my fucking. It didn't take long before he swore, arched his spine, threw his head back, and started spurting all over his chest and belly; I had to grip like a jockey to stay on the ride. I fucked him as hard as I could, pinning him to the bed while he bellowed in the last convulsion of his orgasm—then I kept on fucking him, ten strokes, fifteen, twenty—until I could hold back no longer, and, burying myself as deeply in him as I could, filled him with come.

He held me in place with his legs, which were wrapped around my butt; only when I had gone soft did he relinquish me, and when he did he grasped my head and kissed me as if he would have sucked the breath from me.

I figured my seduction had been a success.

We slept naked that night in each other's arms.

VI

EVERY GREAT DETECTIVE NEEDS A LOYAL ASSISTANT, AND after I'd spent the night "training" Boy Morgan he was every bit as loyal as I could wish. As sidekicks go, he wasn't the brightest—but I comforted myself that even Dr. Watson wasn't always quick off the mark. And Morgan had a great advantage over Watson: he was rapidly learning to take cock up his ass and down his throat, as he demonstrated at first light.

We were just finished, lying naked and covered in semen on sheets that were equally distressed, when there was a knock at the door and, before we had time to tidy ourselves, Burroughs, the butler, entered with a tray. Like all proper English butlers, he was generally imperturbable, though I did notice that his pupils doubled in size as he took in my hairy body and Morgan's smooth one.

"Thank you, Burroughs," I said, hastily arranging a damp sheet around my genitals. "If you'd like to put the tray down..."

Morgan, shielding himself with a hand fore and aft,

nipped off to the bathroom, whooping as he went. Burroughs, nodding his head in assent (and casting one furtive look at Morgan's disappearing rear), placed the tray, containing tea, on the table.

"Your breakfast will be ready in half an hour, sir." He showed no sign of leaving.

"Thank you, Burroughs."

"If that's all, sir..."

"I think so, thank you."

But still he stood at the foot of the bed, his eyes cast down, fighting the desire to stare. I assumed that, if I gave him a flash, he'd be on his way, so I obligingly swung my legs over the side of the bed, allowing him a full view of my hairy ass and my soft cock and everything in between. Anyway, I was parched; and, since living in England, I had learned to appreciate a cup of tea first thing in the morning. I poured; Burroughs remained rooted to the spot.

"Sorry, Burroughs, was there something?"

The poor old man was struggling against a lifetime's training, which told him to make himself scarce, and an overwhelming desire to stay and stare. Surely he didn't think that, while Morgan was in the shower...

"Yes, sir. I must speak to you." I could see from his honest, aged face just how much it cost him to say those words. I took pity on him and grabbed a robe; I figured that, if I covered myself up, Burroughs might find it easier to concentrate on the essential things. Then I remembered his hints of the night before, when we were finishing our port; I had been so intent on getting Morgan to bed that I had not, at the time, taken advantage of a witness who was ripe for questioning. If I was going to become a great detective, I would have to learn to master my own libido.

"Go ahead, Burroughs," I said, lying back on the bed and indicating a chair. He perched on the edge of the seat. "Will you have a cup of tea? Looks like you need one."

"I shouldn't, sir, but under the circumstances..." His hand shook as he poured milk and tea into the cup, from which he sipped like a nervous old lady. Something had rattled his composure, and it wasn't just the sight of two young postcoital athletes.

"So, Burroughs. What's on your mind?"

"I don't like to say, sir..."

"Take your time."

"I'm so worried about Sir James, you see."

"Of course, Burroughs. Sir James had a very distressing day. We're all worried for him."

Whatever he wanted to tell me, he hoped I would guess before he was obliged to say it. Such was the loyalty of servants at that time, I believe Burroughs would have covered up far more than a suspicious death if his own self-interest was not threatened.

"Indeed, sir. Unpleasantness of any sort is so...unwelcome." He sipped his tea again, watching over the top of his glasses. Morgan was singing and splashing around in the shower, absolutely on top of the world; getting fucked suited him.

"Please excuse Boy," I said. "He's in high spirits."

"Apparently so, sir."

"Morgan is a great friend."

"Sir."

"And of course I would be terribly distressed if anything were to happen to him."

"Yes..." Burroughs rested his cup and saucer in his lap and stared out the window.

"Awful to see a pal in a scrape, isn't it, Burroughs?"

"Yes..."

"I mean, if Morgan got into trouble, I'd do anything to help him out. I wouldn't care if I had to break a few rules in order to do so. That's the meaning of friendship, I'd say."

There was silence. Burroughs's eyes were wet; I'd hit the mark.

"Burroughs, is there something you need to tell me?" A tear rolled down his cheek, and he carefully replaced his cup on the tray.

"I'm sorry, sir," he said, taking off his glasses and wiping his eyes with an immaculate handkerchief. "It's been a terrible strain, all of this."

I moved closer to him, just as Boy came bounding out of the bathroom, wet-haired and completely naked, save for a towel slung negligently over his shoulder.

"Hello! He still here? Oh, good, tea. I say, this cup's been..."

"Morgan," I said, "be a good fellow and just sit quietly, would you? Mr. Burroughs has something to tell us."

"Oh, rather. Sorry about that." He threw himself onto the bed, practically bouncing me into Burroughs's lap in the process, and sprawled out.

"And Boy, old chap?"

"Yes, Mitch?"

"If you could just cover yourself up for a moment. You're rather distracting like that."

"'Course. Don't mind me." He pulled a corner of the sheet between his legs to make a sort of loincloth—though Morgan was too active, and too easily distracted, for this to stay in place for long. Soon his cock was lolling out in full view again.

"Now, Burroughs, go on. We're listening. You can trust Boy as you'd trust me."

"Oh, sir, I don't know where to begin..."

I could see this going on all morning, and we were losing precious time. At the rate the police were working, Meeks would be hanged before Burroughs had stammered out his concerns.

"Is it something to do with Mr. Walworth's death?"

"Yes, sir. It's got us all at sixes and sevens..."

"And you're worried that the police have the wrong man."

"By Jove, sir, however did you guess? That's just it. I'm very much afraid they've made a mistake. With the greatest respect to Sir James, of course, and the local officers..."

"Of course they've got the wrong man. Everyone can see that Meeks is innocent. But there's no point in telling them that; it suits everyone to get this cleared up as quickly as possible, and as Meeks isn't making any attempt to defend himself..."

"Oh, the stupid boy, the stupid, stupid boy," Burroughs blurted. "What on earth does he hope to gain by—" He checked himself, unwilling to overstep a certain mark. I would have to play this witness carefully, lest he bolt altogether. Leaning forward, and allowing my robe to fall open to the stomach, I switched into confidential mode.

"What we need, you see, if we're to save Meeks's neck, is evidence of some kind to prove that he was not at the scene of the crime, wherever that may have been, at the time of Mr. Walworth's death."

"An alibi!" Morgan said, full of enthusiasm. "That's the thing!"

"That's just it, sirs," Burroughs said, uncertain whether to look down the front of my robe or to feast his eyes on Morgan's reexposed nakedness. "Poor Charlie Meeks could not have had anything to do with Mr. Walworth's death."

"Why not?"

"Because I know where he was all yesterday afternoon."

"Indeed. And why didn't you say so at the time, when the police were here?"

"He wouldn't hear of it."

"I take it Meeks has something to hide."

Burroughs was silent again, wrestling with some big confession. I lay back on my pillow and, by crooking one leg, gave him an uninterrupted view of my nether regions. Burroughs stared, licked his lips and continued; we had found the key to unlock his evidence.

"Everyone does in this house."

This was the most indiscreet thing Burroughs had said in his entire life, and I noticed that, while he said it, his eyes were boring into Boy Morgan's crotch. Boy had noticed too, and thrust his hips ever so slightly forward. Perhaps he wasn't quite as stupid as I suspected.

"That's very interesting, Burroughs. Yourself included, I suppose."

"Well, sir..."

"How, for instance, are you so certain of Meeks's whereabouts yesterday afternoon, when the murder was committed?"

"I make it my business to know where my staff are."

"And where was Meeks, exactly?"

"Oh, dear..."

Burroughs was clamming up again; Morgan ran a hand over his stomach, where the little patch of hair that led down to his groin was still damp, then pressed the heel of his palm into his pubis, making his cock jump. Burroughs, never letting his eyes wander, continued.

"He was in his room all afternoon."

"How can you be sure of that?"

"I..."

"You were with him, I take it."

"Certainly not!" Burroughs looked quite shocked. Boy closed his eyes and spread his legs.

"That is to say, I know that he was most definitely there. I could swear to it."

"You mean?"

"Yes. I was watching him."

"Watching?"

"I have to keep an eye on the boys sometimes. It's essential to maintain discipline belowstairs."

"Of course." If this little white lie helped Burroughs, it was fine by me—but it was clear that we had a Peeping Tom on our hands.

"Over the years, I've installed a...well, you could call it a surveillance system throughout the staff quarters. It's most necessary."

"And how does it work?"

"I really don't think..." Burroughs began. Morgan rolled over onto his stomach, crooking one leg at ninety degrees. His butt looked good enough to eat. (I well knew that it was.)

"All the servants' rooms are at the back of the house, you see," Burroughs said, in a quiet monotone. "They're arranged over three floors, connected by a spiral staircase. Mrs. Ramage's girls are on the top floor; my young men are on the lower two. You understand, of course, that this is a very problematic situation."

"Hence the need for constant surveillance."

"Precisely. By a rather ingenious arrangement of holes drilled through the walls, I have enabled myself to carry out spot checks on the whereabouts and activities of the indoor staff. It saves no end of trouble."

"I see. And do they know about this?"

"Well, that's a very..." Morgan lifted his hips off the bed and pushed his cock back between his legs. It was half-hard—which, considering the workout it had had in the last 24 hours, surprised me and delighted Burroughs.

"Yes, they know. It's better for all concerned to understand the situation. That means that if anyone is caught out of line, it's a simple disciplinary matter."

"How does that work, Burroughs?"

"You must understand, sir, that I take a fatherly interest in my young men." *Fatherly, my ass*, I thought, but kept it to myself. "I don't wish any of them to get into trouble, but

I'm afraid the proximity of Mrs. Ramage's girls is sometimes too much of a temptation. Well, they're only men, after all."

"I see. And there's been a certain amount of corridor creeping, has there?"

"It has been known. Take young Hibbert, for instance, the second footman. He's a terror. I've told him a thousand times that the upper floor is out of bounds, but he will not listen."

"And what happens when he's caught?"

"I have to punish him, of course."

"And how did you catch him? Do you have spy holes into the girls' quarters as well?"

"Good heavens, no! Perish the thought."

"Perhaps Mrs. Ramage does."

"No, sir, I don't think so. But we hear things. We learn things."

"I'm sorry, Burroughs, but I'm confused. If you don't actually see things, then what's the use of your spy system?"

Burroughs was flustered. The masquerade of "surveillance" had crumbled. He started clearing away tea things. Fortunately, Morgan chose just that moment to roll over onto his back; his cock lay across his thigh, pulsing slightly. Burroughs found the sight calming, and sat down again.

"The thing is, sir, that I'm a very indulgent father to my boys. I can't find it in my heart to turn them out. That Hibbert, for instance. He can wind me round his little finger."

"So if he's naughty with one of the girls, he lets you...play with him?"

"Certainly not, sir." Burroughs sounded wounded but did not seem anxious to leave—especially now that Boy was gently masturbating himself.

"What, then? Come on, Burroughs. I have to know."

"He lets me...see."

"See?"

"See him. On his bed. Through the spy hole."

"I see."

"And he's very kind."

"You mean he puts on a show for you."

"Precisely."

"You like to watch, don't you, Burroughs?"

"Yes, sir."

"Do you like watching what Morgan's doing now, Burroughs?"

"Yes, sir."

"Would you like to see what Morgan and I were doing earlier?"

Burroughs's mouth was dry; he couldn't say the word *yes*, but he didn't need to.

"Tell me everything I want to know, Burroughs, and I'll suck his cock while you watch."

"Yes sir."

"And I'll make him come for you."

"Yes sir."

"Anything else you'd like to see?"

"Perhaps..."

"Yes?"

"If the young gentleman would put his shoes and socks on."

"Morgan?"

Morgan grinned—the filthiest grin I have ever seen in my life—and hastily obliged. I had to agree with Burroughs: there was something delightful about this obscene state of near nakedness. Morgan lay back on the bed and lifted his legs in the air, showing off his footwear.

"Go on, Burroughs."

Burroughs cleared his throat and began.

"It all started, honestly, as a way of keeping the indoor staff under control. We'd had a couple of scandals in Drekeham Hall after the war, you see; girls had to be sent away, and Mrs. Ramage was quick to point the finger at my staff. She was right, of course, but I didn't have the heart to dismiss any of them, so I agreed to take measures to curb any such activities in the future. I installed spy holes in all the rooms—all of them positioned to give me a clear view of the bed and the basin. All I had to do was run up and down the stairs, checking on each room, and I could be certain that my staff were where they should be, when they should be. As for the girls' quarters, Mrs. Ramage took to patrolling the corridors. She has very sharp hearing, Mrs. Ramage does.

"And for a while, it worked very well. We had no more unpleasantness, and Mrs. Ramage was content. She became lazy, trusting. But then, of course, it became so difficult to find staff who could be trusted in the way that one would like. Things started to become so awkward."

"What happened, Burroughs? Tell me, and I'll suck his cock."

The words tumbled out of him. "Well we had some dreadful young man who was up and down those stairs every night, and he was very bad for morale. Taught the others bad ways. But I couldn't turn him out; he was the best footman I ever had, and the family liked him so much. He was connected with Sir James's regiment. No question of dismissal. But what could I do? I had to maintain discipline. Oh, my goodness, sir, that's the way."

I had just taken Morgan's cock to the back of my throat; Morgan was rubbing my head and moaning in delight. With all this going on, it was hard to concentrate on Burroughs's confession—but concentrate I did, I am proud to say. I mumbled some encouragement, though my mouth was full.

"And so I'm afraid I left myself open to corruption of the worst sort. The young man in question persuaded me that he was being careful with the girls, and that there was no chance of any unwanted results, if you understand me, and said that if I would keep quiet and not cause trouble he'd let me watch him when he was alone in his room. And so I did. He was a lovely-looking lad, about your height, sir, and very strongly built, and I could see immediately why he was so popular with the ladies. I believe that he enjoyed putting on a show for me. He always made sure that everything was clearly visible, but he never gave the slightest indication that he knew I was watching. He'd do anything, sir. And the worse his behavior upstairs in the women's quarters became, the more extravagant his performances for me. Dressing up, sir. Putting things up his...well, you know where. Passing water into his chamber pot. And always finishing up by relieving himself right in front of me."

I could feel that Morgan was getting close to coming, so I stopped sucking. There were questions that needed to be asked. I relinquished his cock, and pushed Morgan's hand away as he made to finish himself off.

"So every time one of your staff commits an indiscretion...?"

"That footman was a very bad influence, sir. Before I could do anything about it, he'd spread the word to the rest of the staff. Soon they all knew the price of my silence, and I was spending more time watching them than I was attending to my other duties. The hours were punishing. It was perfectly all right if only one of them was performing for me, but sometimes there were two, or even three. I have to get up at five every morning to prepare for breakfast, sir, and sometimes I wasn't getting to bed much before three."

"Exhausting for you, I'm sure. What happened to that footman?"

"In the end it was he who decided to leave. Ran off with a local girl, leaving an awful lot of broken hearts upstairs."

"But the 'surveillance' continues, clearly."

"Well, sir..."

I spread Morgan's legs and showed Burroughs his pink, freshly washed hole, rubbing it and poking it with my fingers, which I wet with spit.

"They take terrible advantage of an old man's weakness. Hibbert, for example. Completely corrupted by the influence of that footman. One bad apple, you see. I have to discipline him twice a week, sometimes more."

"And he puts on a good show for you, I take it."

"Yes, sir, he's a lovely little performer," Burroughs said, forgetting to sound sad or ashamed. "Beautiful hairy little bum, doesn't mind what he sticks up there. And squirts like a—" Suddenly he collected himself and cleared his throat. I worked a finger up Morgan's ass, right to the knuckle, but still would not allow him to touch himself.

"And what about Meeks? I take it he replaced the previous footman."

"Yes, sir. Well, now, Charlie Meeks. He is like a son to me. He's a good boy. I'm very proud of him."

"So he doesn't give you any cause for complaint?"

"No, sir. Mrs. Ramage's girls are quite safe with Charlie."

"You mean he's...like us?"

"Yes, sir."

"So how do you explain your spying on him, Burroughs?"

"I don't spy on him."

The crunch had come. I needed Burroughs to confess that his rampant voyeurism had gone well beyond any feeble pretense of "disciplining" his staff, and that he had been watching Meeks on the afternoon of the murder.

"But I think you must, Burroughs."

"No, sir."

I pulled my finger out of Morgan's hole and rearranged my robe so that my own thick erection was no longer visible. Morgan looked up, wondering what had happened to the pleasurable sensations; I don't believe he'd been following Burroughs's confession at all.

"You mean, I think, that Meeks doesn't know that you spy on him."

"Sir, I've told you, Charlie is like a son to me."

"Fathers don't spy on their sons jerking off, Burroughs."

He looked uncomfortable. Had I gone too far?

"I resent that remark, Mr. Mitchell."

"I apologize. But the fact remains, I think, that you still use the spy hole into Meeks's room."

"I do not."

"Then how do you know where he was on the afternoon in question?"

"I..."

There I had him.

"Do you want to see Morgan come, Burroughs? How would you like him to come? In my mouth?"

Burroughs shook his head.

"Over himself?"

He nodded.

"You want him to finish himself off while you watch?"

"Yes, sir. Please."

"With his legs in the air, so you can see his shoes and socks?"

"Yes..."

Morgan needed no further instructions, and assumed the position. His hand went to his cock, but I grasped his wrist and prevented any movement.

"Then tell me about Meeks."

"I can't..."

"You must. They'll hang him otherwise."

"Well, sir..."

I let go of Morgan's wrist, and he started stroking himself; this was not going to take long.

"You watch him, don't you?"

"Yes, I do. I love watching him."

"And you saw him yesterday afternoon."

"All afternoon, sir. Oh, God." Morgan was starting to writhe, and allowed one shod foot to hang over the side of the bed, right by Burroughs's chair.

"And you could swear to that?"

"Don't make me, sir."

"Swear to me, Burroughs. I have to know that you saw him there."

"Yes, sir."

"Swear."

"I swear, sir."

And so did Morgan, who let out a quiet, prolonged "Oh, fuck..." before squirting over his stomach and chest. There wasn't much spunk, but enough to keep Burroughs happy.

"Yes sir, I swear it, I was watching him all yesterday afternoon, he was in his room with..."

And then, as Morgan squeezed out the last drops of come from his cock and started rubbing it over his torso, we heard the very last thing in the world that we expected to hear.

From the landing right outside our door, in tones that would have frozen water, came the voice of Lady Caroline Eagle.

"Burroughs! Where are you, Burroughs!"

I leaped off the bed and, dragging a dazed Morgan with me, retreated to the bathroom just before the door burst open. Burroughs busied himself with the tea things. Fortunately for him, he was a consummate actor.

"Lady Caroline?"

"What are you doing in here?"

"I have just served the young gentlemen tea."

I pressed my ear against the bathroom door.

"Where are they?"

"I believe they are dressing, madam."

Right on cue, Morgan flushed the toilet, disposing of yet another wad of sperm-soaked tissue.

"Get downstairs this instant, Burroughs. We need you at breakfast."

There was silence, and I guessed that, unchecked, Lady Caroline's bullying manner could make things very unpleasant for Burroughs. And so I burst through the bathroom door as if I was unaware of any female presence, my robe decently knotted.

"Thanks for that, Burroughs, we'll be down in— Oh, my goodness! Lady Caroline!"

It worked. Confused, embarrassed, and utterly routed, she backed out of the room, muttering something incomprehensible about "the state of the silver."

Burroughs picked up the tray and followed her, winking as he closed the door.

VII

Now, at last, I had a case on my hands rather than just a few random suspicions and a lot of wishful thinking inspired by detective fiction. It was clear that Charlie Meeks, the Eagles' first footman, who was currently being abused in police custody, had not killed the mysterious Reg Walworth. Not, at least, if Burroughs was to be believed—and I saw no reason to doubt the fundamental truth of his testimony. Even if he was untrustworthy on the details, I believed that he had been spying on Meeks at the time of the crime, and had told me in order to exonerate a young man whom he held in high esteem. I believed, in fact, that Burroughs's feelings for Meeks went beyond the paternal butler–footman relationship that he had implied; I recognized something much more like love.

Added to the abuse of Meeks at the police station, his refusal to complain or protest his innocence, the clumsy attempts by Leonard Eagle to divert my suspicions, and the general air of abstraction surrounding Sir James, it made up a very rich stew of suspicion indeed. And what exactly had

Belinda Eagle seen that upset her so much? And why had her brother Rex absented himself from the scene of the crime so rapidly? Why was Lady Caroline so eager to prevent Burroughs from talking? What was the position of Lady Diana Hunt, the frosty heiress who had arrived hotfoot from France as soon as the murder was public knowledge?

I had to find out more, so I dispatched Morgan belowstairs to interview the domestic staff—I figured that his goofy bonhomie would work better with them, as they weren't crazy about foreigners—and I set myself about extracting some information from the person I considered to be the heart of the problem, Sir James Eagle himself. He had been very welcoming when I first arrived at Drekeham Hall, and spoke expansively of his admiration for "the new world," the energy of Americans, our business acumen, and so on and so forth, so I thought it not unreasonable to address myself to him disguised as an eager young scholar eager to drink at the teat of Mother England's ancient wisdom.

This proved easier said than done. Since the events of the previous afternoon, Sir James had withdrawn from family life, making perfunctory, moody appearances at meals and doing little more than grunting in response to any comment. He certainly didn't have time for guests, and had closed himself in his study, where, his secretary said, he was busy working on a speech that he would be making to "the House" about the shocking state of pig farming in his Norfolk constituency. This sounded plausible enough—but it didn't chime with the friendly, affable Sir James I had met a couple of days before, who had actually invited me to his study "any time you want to talk, old chap." That, coupled with a manly clap on the shoulder, emboldened me to press my suit.

The secretary occupied a strange position in the household, welcomed neither belowstairs as one of the domestic staff nor in the family dining room. He lived in his own quarters, a small guest room on the floor above that on which Boy Morgan and I had been billeted. His must have been a very lonely life, and I hoped to capitalize on this by offering the hand of friendship.

"I'm afraid I must get on now," the secretary said, attempting to usher me out of Sir James's outer office. "I have so much correspondence to prepare for Sir James to sign tonight."

He wasn't a bad-looking fellow, though in comparison to Cambridge athletes like Morgan, Rex Eagle, and myself he was a pretty puny specimen. Then again, compared with the feline, slim-hipped Leonard, he was masculine enough. He was slightly balding—just the first stages of hair loss, which gave him a widow's peak of dark-brown hair. He was tall, pale-skinned, and short-sighted; overall, the impression was of a man who spends too much time indoors, and not enough of that time indulging in indoor sports. He can't have been more than a couple of years older than me, but he would have passed for thirty. He wore a white shirt and a stylish herringbone vest and trousers; the jacket was hung neatly over a chair. His tie, with a large Prince of Wales knot, was loosened; these were his only concessions to the warm weather. I was dressed in as little as I could get away with—a short-sleeved shirt and baggy linen trousers.

I was about to leave, conceding defeat in my attempt to penetrate the inner sanctum, when it occurred to me that Sir James's personal secretary might be an even better source of information than Sir James himself, particularly given the young man's parlous position in the household. Surely someone so friendless, so homeless, might be encouraged to talk to an affable young man like me? I thought this was particularly likely when I caught him addressing himself not to my face but to the tuft of black hair that protruded from the V of my shirt.

"It must be great working with a man like Sir James," I

ventured, thinking that it must be anything but. "He's a real force to be reckoned with. Not like the university men, living in an ivory tower. He's in touch with what's going on in the world. I envy you."

The secretary raised his eyebrows a little, but nodded. "Yes, Sir James is an excellent employer. I'm very lucky, as you say."

There was more to this than met the eye, and I remembered Burroughs's statement that everyone in the Eagle household had a secret. Why not this pale-faced, serious young man as well?

"I'd give anything to spend a couple of months in your shoes."

"Oh, would you indeed?" The secretary shot me a look in which sarcasm was mingled with embarrassment. Here was a man clearly not happy with his lot.

"Sure I would. Access to all that real stuff, the powers that be, you know, the things that we never read about in the papers. The stuff that matters."

This time the secretary couldn't contain himself, and let out a noise that is usually transcribed as "Pah!"

"Oh. I guess it's not as much fun as it looks, Mr....sorry, we haven't been properly introduced. I'm Edward Mitchell."

"I know who you are, Mr. Mitchell," he said, taking my extended hand rather gingerly, as if he'd much rather not. His hand was warm and dry, which encouraged me; I feared that, like many bookish men I'd met at college, he would incline to clamminess. "I'm West. Vincent West."

"Pleased to meet you, Vince."

He winced at this familiarity, but at least he was no longer so eager to get me out of the room.

"I'm sorry to disillusion you, Mr. Mitchell," he said, lowering his voice, "because I thought the very same thing when I was your age, about to come out of Cambridge and enter the civil service. I dreamed of stalking the corridors of power, as you say. Of influencing public life from behind the scenes. Well, it didn't quite turn out that way, as you can see."

"Looks good from where I'm standing." Our eyes met, and then, with one accord, each of us dropped his gaze to the other's crotch. It was one of those moments of mutual understanding which never cease to delight me.

"Looks good from here as well," West said in a whisper, blushing furiously. He cleared his throat. "Anyway, Mr. Mitchell, I must get on with this correspondence, or Sir James will have my guts for garters, as they say. But should you have no definite plans for lunch..."

"I don't."

"Then perhaps you would allow me to show you around the house? It's one of my many duties, you see. I conduct tours for visitors, as and when they arrive. Oh, Drekeham Hall is full of historical wonders, very few of them, I might add, gathered by the present incumbents, who bought the whole lot outright a few years ago. Anything you need to ask me, I'll do my best to answer your questions."

"That would be great," I said, shaking him warmly by the hand once again, then refusing to relinquish my grip. We stood close. "I'm eager to learn as much as possible."

"Well, that will certainly make a refreshing change," West said.

The telephone rang, and I left him to answer it.

Morgan had been dispatched belowstairs with a simple brief: to find out as much as he could about anything that was being discussed. To charm, to flirt, to blunder, in short to use his massive personal charms to gather information as a bee gathers pollen. I would sift the dross from the gold, I thought, and use my superior deductive powers to piece together "our" case.

I'd arranged to meet him at the bottom of the garden, near the entrance to the woods into which Leonard had taken me; I thought it was time that Morgan was introduced to the pleasures of the swimming pool. There was time to kill before our eleven o'clock rendezvous, so I took advantage of the beautiful weather and the privacy of the gardens to indulge in a bit of sunbathing. This was something that English people in general did not do; the nearest they got to exposing their flesh to the sun was by donning an elaborate bathing costume. I, however, was accustomed to walking around shirtless at the very least—and I assumed that, with the house being in such uproar, nobody was going to mind a bit of American flesh. I wandered over the formal gardens to an area of lawn that was shielded from the main house by a row of laburnums, stripped off my top, and lay down to relax.

It was a beautiful day, and Drekeham Hall was a beautiful place. The air was as fresh as it could be, a mixture of freshly cut grass, roses, and the all-pervasive tang of the nearby sea. The sky was a deep blue, broken only by a few puffy white clouds that sailed slowly by. Bees buzzed, birds chirped, and, occasionally, a door would slam somewhere in the house. I was too comfortable on my patch of grass, too much in love with the simple pleasures of heat and light, to pay much attention to anyone's comings and goings. If I lifted my head, I could see one of the gardeners in the distance mowing the lawn; so I had him, then, to thank for the delicious perfume in the air. He was doing a beautiful job, mowing in neat up-and-down strips, emptying the clippings in the woodland at the end of every circuit, finally leaning his mower against a tree and wandering off for a well-earned rest.

I tried to concentrate on the case, putting together the few facts that I had so far gathered, but soon I found myself dreaming of the surfeit of sexual pleasures I'd had in the last twenty-four hours. Morgan in the cupboard and in the bathroom, Leonard in the woods, Shipton in the police station "bog," then the whole night and the morning with Morgan and our little impromptu display for Burroughs—not to mention the guilty pleasure of watching Piggott's fat, veiny club of a cock pushing up and down against Meeks's handsome, martyred face...

Suddenly the sun went away, and something hard and sharp dug into my crotch. I braced myself for fight or flight—but, looking up, I saw that I was under attack by nothing more sinister than Boy Morgan, who stood looking down at me with an expression of amused contempt, stirring my balls with the toe of his shoe.

"Forgive me for not waiting all bloody morning," he said, "but it's nearly twenty past eleven. So much for our date."

"Oh, shit," I said, sitting up and feeling distinctly woozy from too much sun. "I must have drifted off."

"I hope you were dreaming about me," he said. "If anyone else makes you that stiff, I might get jealous." And he was right; I was as stiff as a pole in my pants, as I often am on waking from slumber. It subsided quickly as I jumped to my feet.

"So," I said, trying to regain the upper hand, "what have you found out for me?"

"A lot more than you've found out, lying there dreaming of you-know-what," he said. "Come on, let's get you into the shade."

I found the path that twisted into the woods, through the rhododendron thickets to the secret pond. Morgan was delighted, and started to strip with whoops of joy.

"That's more like it!" he said, flinging his clothes far and wide. "I'm sick of this stuffy bloody hole and the stuffy bloody people that live in it. I'm going to swim."

I was in like a shot after him, and we wasted more time in fighting and diving and splashing like a couple of otters. Finally tired of the game, we lay at the edge of the pond, both naked. I was propped against the pond's grassy edge; Morgan's head lay on my stomach. The water, lapping on my sunburned skin, felt like heaven.

"This is the life," Morgan said, as I ran my fingers through his wet hair. "God, what a bloody miserable place this is. So beautiful, they've got all the money in the world, they've got all this"—he gestured around him—"and yet they're all down in the dumps."

"Says who?"

"Says everyone you talk to. Now listen to this, Mitch. I got chatting to the kitchen maid, nice enough girl, nothing much to look at but she's got a fantastic pair of tits. Doesn't have to work too hard, just does a bit of washing up, bit of cooking, bit of cleaning, she has a much better life than most of the girls of her position I've known, and I've known a few." He started toying with his cock at this point; obviously I would never convert him entirely to my way of thinking.

"Anyway, what I'm trying to say is, she's got nothing much to complain about, and the chef is a nice old bloke, French, of course, but perfectly decent all the same. Well, the moment I had said 'hello' to her and come up with some cock-and-bull story about getting lost on the way to the garden, she was off. Bloody this, bloody that, unfair this, unfair that. Can't stand the housekeeper. Can't stand the footman. Can't bloody stand the bloody butler; hates him with a vengeance, the little minx. Didn't take much to find out why, either. He's come between her and her true love. I could have told you that. Turns out she's been seeing that young Hibbert fellow who came and picked us up at the station."

"Oh, the good-looking, dark-skinned one? Yes, he has a bit of a reputation belowstairs."

"Suppose you wouldn't mind having a go at finding out why, eh?" Morgan said, grinning up at me and splashing a bit of water in the general direction of my face. "Anyway, big Susie the kitchen maid reckons that the only thing that's standing between her and marrying Mr. Hibbert and finding a decent position as a housekeeper and butler in their own right is our friend Burroughs. By the way, I hope he enjoyed the show this morning."

"I certainly did."

"Yes, well I could see that, you randy bastard. But I noticed that he never touched himself. Couldn't even see any sign of a stiffie. Do you think the old boy's past it?"

"Past certain things, maybe, but his brain is still functioning even if his cock isn't."

"Oh, well. We brought the old fellow a bit of happiness, I suppose. I didn't mind. Rather liked it, actually. Other chaps looking at me and all that. Suppose you've noticed I sometimes get stiff in the changing rooms after rowing."

"Yeah, I had noticed something like that. Stop talking about your cock, Morgan, or I'll have to fuck you again."

"Christ, don't know if I'm ready for that yet—my arse is feeling a bit tender after last night. Mind you—look at that! Part of me is interested."

His cock, like mine, was well on the way to being stiff. Time to change the subject before, once again, sex got the upper hand.

"Who else did you talk to down there?"

"I had a word with Hibbert, of course."

"Oh, yes."

"He's got no time for Meeks either, though he was a good deal more charitable about Burroughs, as you might expect. But as for Meeks; no, he's glad to see the back of him. Wants his position, I suppose, which you can understand, but there was more to it than that. Nothing he'd come right out and say. Things like 'ideas above his station' and 'class traitor,' that sort of thing. I suspect Mr. Hibbert is a bit of a Bolshevik."

"Maybe. But I'm beginning to wonder about Charlie

Meeks. Why him? Why would anyone imagine that he was a killer? Why is everyone so eager to get rid of him?"

"And why does Burroughs love him so much, apart from the obvious?"

"Why, indeed. Go on."

"That was it, really. Oh, and I saw that poor hall boy, Simon. Sweet kid. Grinned from ear to ear when he saw me coming, but couldn't tell me much. Deaf as a post and can't talk properly. Showed me some nasty burns on his wrists; chef said the poor little sod was always hurting himself, carrying bedpans and laying fires, that sort of thing. I would have liked to help him out, actually. But it was nearly eleven, and some of us had appointments to keep."

"Tell me more about the burns. What were they like?"

"Just round his wrists. Looked a bit sore, really. Must have touched hot metal, something like that."

"On both wrists?"

"Yes. Doesn't seem very likely, does it?"

"Not at all. I suspect Simon knows more than he can tell."

"I'd better have another word with him."

"Sounds like you're rather eager to get to know our little hall boy."

"Jealous, Mitch?"

"Of him? No."

"Of whom, then?"

"Who do you think?"

"Come on, not jealous of Belinda, are you?"

"A bit."

"Well you're bloody mad, then."

"Am I?"

"Look, Mitch. Belinda is a lovely girl. And yes, I'm in love with her and I'm going to marry her. It's the real thing, not like Rex and that bloody awful ice maiden he's marrying for all the wrong reasons, just to please Mum and Dad, if you ask me. No, I love Billie and we're going to have a family. But that doesn't mean that you and I aren't going to be great pals, does it? Doesn't mean we won't have fun. I mean, we've already done a hundred times more in the last twenty-four hours than Billie and I have done in a year and a half."

"Okay."

"So stop worrying and start applying your great mind to the matter in hand."

I was about to cement this new entente by sucking his dick, when the summer silence was broken by the sound of thundering hooves and a horse neighing at close quarters. The woods, it seemed, were not quite as secret as Leonard had led me to believe.

Morgan and I lay low, our heads barely peeping over the grassy bank of the pool. The hooves pounded nearer, and through the dark leaves and branches we could see flashes of a brown flank, a tossing mane and tail. And then it broke into the clearing around the pool, a handsome chestnut mare—and riding on its back were two naked men.

Once we had recovered from the shock of this dream-like apparition, Morgan and I padded off in the direction in which the horse had disappeared. The ground was covered with dead leaves and twigs, so we had to move carefully so as not to make too much noise—but once we reached the shelter of the rhododendron bushes, beneath which nothing settled or grew, we could proceed faster, if less comfortably, as we were obliged to bend and duck to avoid the branches. Both of us were fleet of foot, and it gave me great pleasure to watch Morgan's buttocks jiggling a few feet ahead of me.

Suddenly he stopped and gestured for silence. I could hear the unmistakable sound of the horse grazing, tearing up mouthfuls of grass, and occasionally stamping a hoof or snorting. And I could hear laughter.

Morgan crept toward the edge of the bushes, the side

farthest from the house, which gave onto a strip of untended field that, after fifty yards or so, crumbled into cliffs. We crouched shoulder to shoulder, blinking out into the dazzling sunshine. Flies buzzed around us, landing on our shoulders.

There was the horse, untethered and grazing at will. And there, between us and the horse, perhaps only fifteen feet away, were its two naked riders.

One of them I recognized—the gardener whom I had seen mowing the lawn. He had close-cropped black hair, and looked as if he might be of Mediterranean extraction, with olive skin that tanned easily. I had an uninterrupted view of his face as he lay in a half-seated position, his hands behind his head, his neck and shoulders raised from the ground, which tensed his abdominal muscles.

I couldn't see his companion at first, until I noticed some movement in the long grass, something dark and hairy bobbing around a few inches beneath the gardener's belly. It was a head.

The gardener's eyes were closed, and he was thoroughly enjoying his midmorning blow job. Morgan and I were enjoying it too; after a few moments of spying on this private moment, we were both erect, though there was little we could do about it without drawing attention to our presence.

After a while, the gardener reached down and drew his friend up to his level. At first I thought the second man was wearing an undershirt, a jersey of some sort—but then, on more careful inspection, I realized that he was just very, very hairy. Now, I'm on the hairy side, and even at twenty I had more hair on my chest and stomach than any of my contemporaries in college. But this fellow made me look positively glabrous. Short, dark hair curled on his shoulders, his neck, and down his back, where it lay glossy against his flanks. When the young man turned around, I saw what appeared to be a doormat on his chest, with two pink nipples poking through. His face, when it was revealed, was heavily stubbled—just a morning's growth, I assumed—and above his eyes was a single, continuous brow. The hair on his head was a rich, dark brown, much the same color as the horse he'd ridden in on.

"It's the groom," whispered Morgan in my ear. "I've seen him at the stables."

The two young men, unaware that they were being observed, sat together in the grass, kissing and stroking each other; I had the impression, from the obvious intimacy between them, that this was no casual, spur-of-the-moment fuck, but a regular liaison. I felt bad watching them—but not so bad that I was about to tear myself away. Besides which, Morgan had me rooted firmly to the spot, having worked a wet finger up my hole. This had the effect of making my cock dribble.

The groom stood up—and I was tickled to see that, far from being totally naked, he was still wearing a pair of dirty old black riding boots. He stood with his hands on his hips, allowing us to see that the pelt of hair went from the line around his neck to which he shaved, all the way to his legs. His nipples, his hands, his upper arms, and his cock were the only parts of him that were not hairy—and their relative nakedness drew more attention than usual to these interesting parts. His cock was long, fatter in the middle than at either end; looming against the summer sky, it looked not unlike a zeppelin emerging from a hairy cloud.

The gardener soon had it safely imprisoned in his mouth and, kneeling at his friend's feet, proceeded to give a blow job that even I would have been proud to administer. Here was someone who had evidently had as much practice in the art as me, and possibly had an even greater natural flair for it. The groom clasped the gardener's head, and they stared into each other's eyes.

Morgan was fucking me with two fingers now, and I had

the distinct impression that he wanted to have more than just fingers in me; so far he had only taken the passive role in our sexual adventures, and I was pleased to see that he wanted to turn the tables. I was torn between the desire to continue watching the show and the desire to drag Morgan back indoors and let him do his worst. As I was pondering this difficult choice, the young man in the boots pulled his dick out of his friend's mouth and squirted a huge load of come in his face—one of the biggest loads I have ever seen. The gardener closed his eyes and, mouth open, took all of it. Some of it landed on his tongue, some on his cheeks, his eyelids, and his chin, and from there it ran down his neck. Thus garnished, he lay back, pumped his hand in his groin a few times, and let go of his own load—and I swear I saw semen jumping above the level of the tall grass. The lovers lay back and disappeared from view, and I was left with nothing to concentrate on but the sensation of Morgan's two fingers battering the walls of my ass.

Time had flown by—and I suddenly realized that lunchtime was approaching. I was about to pry myself unwillingly off Morgan's fingers and hasten back to the pool to collect my clothes when, to my horror, I saw the two fellows getting up from their improvised bed in the grass—and walking straight toward us. I had no choice but to stay put, holding my breath and desperately thinking up some plausible lie that would explain our naked presence.

The gardener and the groom approached the rhododendrons—and stopped, just inches from us. Fortunately, the sun was behind us, dazzling their eyes and not revealing our position, otherwise we would have been discovered for sure. But instead of proceeding through the bushes, they stood there, side by side—and started pissing in unison. Two long, thick streams of urine hit the dark, dusty green leaves of the rhododendrons; a few drops splashed through to where Morgan and I were hiding, sprinkling us with a fine golden mist. We could not move (I for one didn't want to); we just had to keep quiet and watch.

The two boys were in a playful mood, and splashed their piss all over the bushes. The gardener aimed at his friend's boots; this led to a certain amount of fighting, though the streams of piss remained undiminished. Finally they finished and, in a rather touching gesture, shook the last drops off each other's prick. Then they raced each other back to the horse, bounded onto its back, and trotted off.

When they were safely out of earshot, Morgan and I looked at each other and burst into laughter. He pulled his fingers out of my hole, kissed me on the lips (heedless of the fine mist of piss on my face), and dragged me to my feet.

"Come on," he said. "We'd better bathe."

VIII

Vincent West was pacing anxiously in the marbled vestibule, looking at his watch, pretending to take an interest in the statues dotted around the place. Clearly he was not encouraged to show himself in public parts of the house; his existence was eked out in Sir James's office and his own bachelor quarters. I dashed in from the garden, slightly out of breath; the shock of bathing, dressing quickly, and running across the lawn on such a hot afternoon had taken its toll. I checked myself quickly in one of the huge, gilt-framed mirrors that lined the walls, making sure that I didn't look too sex-crazed—I didn't want to frighten West away. Looking at him now, as he paced the hall, not knowing he was observed, I saw a curious mixture of energy and restraint—a man who longed for excitement, affection, and status but who was forced by circumstance to curb his desires.

"Mr. West."

He spun on his heel. "Thought you weren't coming. Let's go. I hate this bloody museum."

Looking around him, he opened the front door (I suspect

that, as staff, he was not meant to use it) and ushered me quickly through.

"Where are we going? Aren't you going to show me around the house?"

"Not bloody likely. We're going to the pub. If I don't get out of this madhouse, they'll have to lock me up for good."

He closed the door behind us and jogged across the gravel of the drive. Released from his prison, he suddenly looked five years younger. What kept a man of such potential in these straitened circumstances?

As soon as we were through the gates, West relaxed. A smile broke through the habitual gloom of his countenance, and for the first time I realized that he was a handsome man.

"What a beautiful day!" he said, turning around and looking at the sky, the hedgerows, and the sea beyond. "Sometimes I never see the outside world for days at a time. Shouldn't be out here today. Sir James is keeping me close by him with a lot of useless bloody correspondence to his constituents. Funny that it should suddenly be so urgent."

Mr. West, clearly, was in an indiscreet mood. I had little to do but to let him talk.

"Pig farming, grazing rights, motor vehicle access, all those subjects that he cares about so deeply." He had picked up a stick and was whacking viciously at the cow parsley that fringed the road. "I've had enough of it all. God, I need a beer."

At the pace that West was setting, we reached the village in less than ten minutes, during which time he had vented his spleen. I bought beer and sandwiches, which we took out into the pub's garden, a perfect confection of geraniums and fuchsias and marigolds. We found a spot under a tree and sat down for our picnic. West took a great draft of beer, wiped the foam from his lips, and finally relaxed.

"Thanks for the treat," he said. "Can't pay you back, I'm

afraid. Not on my wages. Have to take what I can get. It's not a nice position for a man to be in, but there's no point in beating about the bush. I'm very grateful. You're the first person I've been able to talk to since... Well, never mind. Cheers, Mr. Mitchell."

"Mitch."

He grinned again. Mr. West, the Confidential Secretary, had vanished, and in his place was a friendly, bookish young man with broad shoulders and a slim waist.

"And I suppose, if you absolutely insist, you can call me Vince."

We clinked our pint mugs and drank for a moment in silence. His expression darkened again.

"I hope you don't think I'm being disloyal...."

"To whom? To Sir James?"

"Precisely. But I feel I must speak to somebody."

"I'm all ears."

"I thought, when you arrived, that you might be... sympathetic."

This was the sort of coded Anglicism that I had long since learned to translate. "Oh, believe me, Vince," I said, placing a hand discreetly on his, "I'm extremely sympathetic." He beamed at the contact, and the sympathy, and allowed my hand to rest on his.

"What is it that you want to tell me?"

"It's about this business."

"Of course."

"There's something wrong about it all."

"You can say that again."

"Oh!" he said, with great relief, his eyes shining. "So it's not just me! I began to think that solitude was turning me into one of those delusional types who see conspiracies all around them."

"What do you suspect?"

"It's to do with Rex."

"Rex? What's he got to do with anything?"

"Ah. Well, that's a long story. It all goes back to Cambridge."

"All roads around here seem to lead to Cambridge."

"Of course, you're a Cambridge man, aren't you Mitch? And your friend Mr. Morgan. We like Mr. Morgan very much here at Drekeham Hall. He's considered quite a catch for Miss Belinda." He mimicked the mincing intonations of Lady Caroline.

"When did you graduate, Vince?"

"Mmmm..." He took another swig of beer. "Sore point. I didn't graduate. I was...you know."

"Sent down?"

"Yes. There was a scandal. I shared rooms with Rex Eagle when he first came up, and I was in my second year. Our families have some distant connection, so it seemed natural—you know how cliquey Cambridge is. I had been running around with what they called a rather fast set. Would-be poets, would-be musicians, would-be communists, you know the sort."

"I certainly do." And I'd fucked a lot of them—though I didn't feel the need to add this at the time.

"Well, you know how young men can be. There were parties. Rex didn't approve when I brought that crowd to my rooms—he was more interested in rowing and studying. But after a while he got a taste for it, for jazz records and cocktails and...conversation."

"So you and Rex became good friends."

"We did."

"Harry Morgan and I are good friends."

"I imagined you were."

"Very good friends."

"Precisely. As were Rex Eagle and I." He stressed the past tense.

"And then there was a blowup?"

"The college authorities had their eye on our staircase for some time. I don't know who had blown the whistle. The parties were nothing out of the ordinary, far less riotous than the hearties were having. We never smashed anything. But somebody knew what was going on after the parties were over. Someone objected to my friendship with Rex Eagle. And so I was hauled up on some ridiculous charge, and sent down before I could defend myself."

"What did Rex do?"

"Oh, Rex was thoroughly decent. Rex said all the right things, expressed his sympathy, said he could get me a job with his father, which he did, of course. He didn't know it was going to be worse than a prison sentence. At least in prison one might get... Well, no, that's an unworthy thought. He was doing his best. And I was grateful for the position; there aren't many openings for a young man who's blotted his copybook like that. You know what the college dons are like; they smile, and wish you luck, and then they make sure that everyone in the world knows that you're a thoroughly bad egg. I hoped to practice law, or become an academic, but those doors were suddenly closed to me. And so here I am."

"But surely you and Rex..."

"Rex is kind and friendly, and nothing more. Whatever was between us is in the past, he's made that quite clear. The indiscretions of youth. Anyway, he has his lady love."

"Diana Hunt."

"Precisely. Whopper Hunt. Who brings a whopping great fortune into the Eagle coffers just when they need it most."

"So I gather."

"And Rex, you know, is terribly in love with her." Sarcasm dripped from his voice.

"So much in love," I added, "that he ran up to town on business when he knew that she was coming over from France to see him."

"Ah, you know that! Well, that's pretty much par for the course. Rex loves Diana, Diana loves Rex, that's all we're told, and we don't ask questions. But I know Rex, I know him better than he knows himself. I remember those months in Cambridge even if he pretends he doesn't. He could never be happy with Diana Hunt."

"Or with any woman?"

"That's my belief."

"There are some young men who could be happy with both." I was thinking of Morgan, of course.

"We know the sort, don't we? But I don't believe that's true of Rex. He said things to me in our time together—things from the heart. Oh, not about me. I don't flatter myself that he was in love with me. In love with what we could do together, with what I could teach him. But not with me. And I wasn't in love with him, really. He was beautiful, the perfect young blond Apollo, a warrior on the playing fields, a bright student, the most popular young man of his year. Rich, well brought up, with a famous father. Everyone adored him, and it was me who got him. So of course I fancied myself head over heels. But I wasn't. Rex is beautiful, but he is not trustworthy. He is a coward. He denied me, he denied himself. No; any romantic illusions are long gone."

"And how does all of this relate to what happened yesterday?"

"I don't know for certain, but it does. Something has been brewing for a long time. This is the crisis."

"You must be more specific than that, Vince, if I'm going to be of any assistance."

"If anyone knew I was talking to you, they'd fire me. They'd probably put me in prison. Sir James has great influence."

"So I've seen. The local police seem very eager to do his bidding."

"Precisely."

"And now an innocent man will hang."

"Mr. Meeks."

"Yes. He's in Drekeham Police Station, and they're not exactly treating him with kid gloves."

West stared gloomily at the bottom of his empty pint glass.

"Look, damn it all, I can't let this happen, not if I know something that will set things to rights. It's too late to help myself, and I don't really care what happens to me now. But this is all wrong."

"Tell me everything."

He took a deep breath; this was costing him a lot. "Last year Sir James was implicated in a financial scandal. It was suggested that he had taken bribes from some of his business associates to ask questions in the House, in an attempt to discredit a piece of legislation that would have restricted their ability to trade outside the Empire. Sir James insists this was not true, but the mud stuck—and he had to pay a hell of a lot of people a hell of a lot of money for the whole dirty business to be hushed up and forgotten."

"How much money?"

"I don't know the figures, but it was enough to put a serious drain on Sir James's personal fortune. Putting it bluntly, the family is broke."

"But his business friends..."

"Oh, no. Rats desert the sinking ship. They had to distance themselves from him, obviously. So now he's in queer street. No funds. Flat as a pancake."

"Which is why Rex's marriage is so important."

"Lady Diana will bring not only a massive dowry, but also connections. The Hunts are big news in British manufacturing. If Sir James is allied with them, he can laugh in the face of his detractors. He's a made man—again. So nothing must stand in the way of Rex's marriage."

"But what does this have to do with the death of Reg Walworth?"

"That's just what I can't understand. None of it makes sense. Mr. Walworth—well, he was on the payroll for a while, I believe he worked for a firm of builders who made improvements to Sir James's London flat, the one he uses when parliament is sitting. He retained him for a while to complete the work. I understand he had brought him to Drekeham in order to discuss the restoration of the library wing."

"And what does he have to do with Meeks?"

"With Meeks? Nothing whatsoever."

"I understood Meeks invited him."

"No. Absolute rot. Who told you that?"

"Leonard, of course."

"Fucking Leonard!" West's face went red with anger. "That snake!"

"I see he's no friend of yours."

"He's made my life a misery ever since I got here, with his taunts and snide remarks, the little shit. If I could get my hands round that scrawny neck..."

"Come on. Let's go for a walk." I was concerned that one or two other lunchtime drinkers were beginning to glance over at West's outburst. I returned the glasses to the bar and we strolled back to the house.

"But why would they want to get Meeks out of the way?" I asked, trying to fit together the pieces of an insane jigsaw puzzle. "And how did Reg Walworth meet his death? The two things seem completely unconnected."

"Search me," West said, rapidly returning to his gloomy, "official" persona as we neared the house. "But there is a connection. There must be. Sir James's financial difficulties, Rex's marriage to Diana, the death of Mr. Walworth, and the arrest of Meeks."

"And Rex's business trip to London? What's that all about?"

"I have no idea. Rex's 'business' is a mystery to me. He often goes up for a few days, running errands for his father, I suppose. But it's the timing that bothers me. As if he were clearing out for a reason."

We had reached the gates of Drekeham Hall; West was gloomy and silent. I knew that I might not get another chance to speak to him.

"Vince—I want to help you."

"Very decent of you, Mr. Mitchell, but I'm beyond help."

"Crap. I want to get you out of here. Out of Drekeham. Out of England."

"To be honest, Mitch, I'd be happy if you'd just get me out of my pants." He smiled sadly; it was the first time he'd acknowledged his own sexual needs. My cock instantly stiffened, and I began looking around for a shady nook.

"It's too late for that," he said. "Sir James is in his office. Look." I could see the magisterial silhouette against the window. "But thanks."

"I won't let you down," I said, wondering how on earth I could help this troubled soul.

"Don't worry about me, Mitch. But try and save Meeks."

"One more thing, Vince. What do you know about Simon?"

"The hall boy? Nothing. Why?"

"Have you ever spoken to him?"

"No. Not much point, is there? Nice looking, but you know...not all there."

"Is that true?"

"Sometimes he comes up to me and starts grunting away. Can't make out a word. Poor chap's simple."

"How often has he done that?"

"Often enough, particularly recently."

"As if he wanted to tell you something?"

"I suppose. Oh, crikey, have I been a fool?"

"I think we've all been fooled, Vince. Now get upstairs before Sir James sees you. I'll come and see you later. I know where your room is."

I watched West bounding up the stairs two at a time, and no sooner had I turned to go in search of Morgan than I came face to face with Leonard Eagle, who had crept up noiselessly behind me. I remembered what West had called him—a snake—and for a moment I imagined I saw something reptilian in his slender, sinuous form, his dead eyes, his smiling mouth.

"Missssster Mitchell." Was it my imagination, or did he hiss?

"Mister Eagle."

"I see you've been fraternizing with the lower orders."

"Is there a law against it?"

"Not at all! We're very democratic here at Drekeham Hall."

"Not what I would call democracy, Mr. Eagle."

"Ah, those New World ideas again, Mr. Mitchell. We do our best, we do our best. Yours is such a young country..."

"Did you want something?"

"I did, as a matter of fact." I knew what he wanted, and it was staying firmly inside my trousers. If anyone was going to get it, it would be Morgan, or West, or my friend Bill at the police station, or Simon, the hall boy, or even the fat kitchen maid with the wonderful tits—but Leonard Eagle was never getting it again.

"Perhaps you'd like to take a postprandial stroll in the gardens."

"Not today, thank you."

"Don't worry, Edwina," he whispered, grasping my upper arm in his clawlike hand. "Your lily-white ass is quite safe with me. We need to talk."

Everyone in this house needed to talk, it seemed. And everyone was contradicting everyone else.

"Come to my room. Don't worry, I shan't pounce. Not directly after lunch. So bad for my digestion. Besides, I have a friend in the stables who fucked me ragged all morning. And he's twice the man you are."

"Thank you so much."

"A simple question of dimension, Mr. Mitchell. Here we are." He led me up the stairs and opened a door off the first landing—a door close to the cupboard where our story began. Inside was a large, bright room that looked out onto the garden through two huge full-length windows. The furniture was draped with Indian shawls, the surfaces cluttered with bibelots; it was exactly the sort of "aesthetic" decor I had seen (and loathed) a hundred times in Cambridge. The focal point of the room was a large divan, stacked with cushions, upon which, I felt sure, Leonard had disported himself many times.

"Welcome to my humble abode," he said. "My kingdom within a kingdom. I can relax here."

"It's very nice."

"And so private."

"I'm sure."

"You see, I have this lovely sitting room, and my bedroom, and my bathroom, all tucked away from the family."

"That must suit you very well."

"Oh, it does, Mr. Mitchell. Marvelous for entertaining."

"Of which you do a great deal, I'm sure."

"Well, one does one's utmost to spread a little happiness." That's not all he'd spread, of that I was certain.

"Yesterday, for instance, while the rest of you were playing that silly game of Sardines..."

"Oh, yes."

"You wouldn't have known, would you, that we were having quite a private party in here."

"Were you, indeed."

He threw himself onto the divan and reclined like a movie star, drawing a cigarette from his case.

"Got a light, sailor?"

I obliged. I could feel myself once again being drawn into Leonard's web of seduction, and remembered the extraordinary sensations of his rectum on my cock, not to mention the spitting serpent that lay coiled inside his pants. I fought the image down, and thought instead of Meeks's neck in a noose.

"Well, it was a marvelous party."

"Good for you."

"You'd be surprised how democratic we can be."

"Meaning?"

"I draw my guests from all ranks, you see. A couple of pals from London who motored down...actors...no, you didn't meet them, I don't present them to the family. And they brought some friends. A stevedore I believe one of them was, though I have no idea what one of those is, and a stagehand from Collins Music Hall. Do you know Collins? Marvelous place..."

"No."

"What a shame. And then, of course, Mr. Meeks."

"Here? Yesterday afternoon?"

"Oh, yes."

"I don't think so."

"Why not? How would you know where he was?"

I could not betray Burroughs, and had to think fast. "The indoor staff had the afternoon off, didn't they?"

Leonard laughed. "Precisely. You don't imagine he was working, do you? Serving tea and sandwiches while the rest of us fucked each other's brains out? Is that how you think it works? Dear me, no. Mr. Meeks was invited as a guest."

"I see."

"If you don't believe me..."

"Go on. Who else?"

"And of course he brought his friend."

"Reg Walworth."

"Poor Mr. Walworth."

"So it was here that..."

"Not precisely here. In the bathroom, I'm afraid. Something unfortunate happened with a leather belt that became tightened round Mr. Walworth's neck. I believe that some people enjoy the sensations it produces...and others enjoy inflicting them."

"You mean Meeks strangled him?"

"Not deliberately, I'm sure. Mr. Walworth was far too handsome to murder deliberately. But that, alas, is what happened."

I felt it politic to believe him. "And while that was going on in the bathroom, what were you up to?"

"Well, the rest of us—me, Rodney, Neville, and their two rough friends, were amusing ourselves in the bedroom with another young guest. A very accommodating young guest..."

Light dawned.

"You mean Simon, don't you?"

For once, I'd got the better of Leonard Eagle. It was a hunch, but something about Morgan's tale of Simon's wounded wrists, and West's suggestion that the hall boy had sought his confidence before, suggested that the boy was being taken advantage of. For a second, Leonard dropped the mask and looked astonished; then he rapidly regained his composure.

"Ah, you took my tip, did you, and gave him a go? Isn't he lovely? So obliging. You have me to thank for that. I've trained him well."

I went along with it, licking my lips. "You sure have."

Leonard thought he'd won, and became indiscreet. "Well, yesterday we had him tied hand and foot to the four-poster bed next door. Face up, face down. We all had a go at him. He loved it. Moaning away like a little whore."

"Show me the bed."

He opened a door, and there was the bedroom, a clashing horror of chinoiserie and theatrical rags, with a massive old four-poster dominating the floor. Ropes were still attached at each corner; rough, hempen ropes that would easily burn skin.

"Pity you weren't here, Mitch. You'd have enjoyed it."

"Hmmmm."

"If you like, you can tie me up and have a go."

"Not directly after lunch, thanks. Gives me a pain."

"Maybe later, then?" He had that strange, golden sparkle in his eyes again; I guessed that the rough fucking administered by his friend in the stables had started to wear off. I disliked Leonard Eagle intensely, but I could not help recognizing that here was a man with a libido as strong as mine, and even fewer scruples about how he satisfied it.

"Maybe." I thought it best to keep him sweet—and besides, I wasn't entirely averse to the idea of having him bound and at my mercy.

"Neville and his friend had him at both ends."

"Great."

"So you see, we're a very generous family. Generous to our staff. Simon got everything he could have wanted, and more. It's a tradition in Drekeham Hall. Everyone has a go with everyone else, from the lowliest hall boy all the way up to...well, anyway, we had a marvelous time. You must come down when I'm having one of my weekends."

"Perhaps when all this has blown over."

"Yes, precisely. When order has been restored. Quite honestly, I will be glad when Mr. Meeks is out of the way. He's nearly spoiled everything. Stupid boy, getting ideas above his station. But you see, it would be in nobody's interest to let all this blow up in the newspapers. Best if it's..."

"Hushed up? I understand."

"I knew you would. We have to be so careful, don't we?" He ran his hand down my chest and let it rest on my lower abdomen.

I turned and walked out of the room to avoid punching him.

IX

There comes a point in most Sherlock Holmes stories when the great detective takes Watson to one side and tells him that he has divined the truth behind the mystery, then demonstrates his superior powers of deduction by unraveling the entire story to the astonished sidekick (and reader). I felt that the time had come for me to do something of the kind, and had even fantasized about Morgan's starstruck admiration, which he would express in the only way he knew how.

But there was a fly in the ointment. I didn't have a clue what was going on in Drekeham Hall. I had gathered a great deal of information, but I could not, for the life of me, resolve it into a coherent picture. The truth, surely, was right under my nose, but I could not see it. Images were whirling around in my brain: Meeks and Walworth in Leonard Eagle's bathroom; Simon, the hall boy, bound hand and foot, with a cock up each end; Burroughs, the butler, and his network of spy holes... I needed to introduce some order into this erotic jumble, so I went up to my room for a bit of peace and quiet, fully intending to work it all out on a piece of paper and come to a blinding conclusion.

Morgan had had much the same idea. I found him sitting in an armchair, staring out across the gardens. He didn't even turn around when I came in.

"There goes the groom, taking Sir James's hunter for a gallop in the lower field," he said. "Wish I was out there with him."

"What, the hairy one?"

"Yes. The one who just pissed in our faces."

"How many other men work in the stables?"

"None. Just him. They don't have many horses nowadays. Used to be some excellent hunting round here, but Sir James has run it down over the last season or so. Pity, really."

"Just him... I see."

"Is it important?"

"Just another piece of the jigsaw that doesn't fit. If he's the only one in the stables, then he couldn't have been in two places at one time this morning, could he?"

"No. Nobody can do that."

"And yet it seems that everyone in Drekeham Hall can do exactly that. The groom was in the field with the gardener, we watched them, and yet at just the same time he was meant to be fucking Leonard Eagle."

"Impossible."

"Exactly. And you saw how much spunk he shot over the gardener's face."

Morgan grinned. "Gallons of the stuff. Looked like he hadn't come in days."

"Then they rode off together, and it was lunchtime. How was lunch, by the way?"

"Ghastly. I missed you. Everyone's in such a sulk."

"Who was there?"

"Sir James, as gloomy as ever. Lady Caroline, who

looked as if she was about to go to pieces. Whopper Hunt, who barely ate a thing. Billie, who's bearing up wonderfully under the circumstances, but looked like she'd been crying. And of course that awful cove, Leonard."

"Ah. Leonard. It all comes back to Leonard. So he ate lunch with you?"

"Yes."

"Then there's no way he could have snuck in a quickie with the groom."

"Oh, no, definitely not. Besides, he spent most of dinner dropping things under the table and trying to feel my leg. He's a disgusting creature."

"So everything he's told me is a lie."

"Of course it is, Mitch. I could have told you that."

"You don't know what he's told me."

"I don't have to know. Leonard Eagle is a bad egg. Incapable of telling the truth. Everyone knows that."

"In that case..."

And so I related to Morgan everything that Leonard had told me: the party in his quarters, while the rest of us were out of the way playing a silly game of Sardines; the circumstantial evidence of the abuse of Simon, the hall boy; the "actor pals" from London and their rough trade friends—and Meeks's unexpected taste for dangerous forms of gratification that had cost Reg Walworth his life.

"But what about Burroughs? He said that Meeks was in his room all afternoon."

"And I'm sure he was. But if it comes to evidence, whom are the police going to believe? Sir James's brother, backed up by Sir James himself, no doubt? Or a couple of visitors to the house who can't tell how they got their evidence, and who have no right to be sticking their noses in in the first place? Oh, it's all been very carefully, cleverly sewn up."

"But the thing is, Mitch, it's a pack of lies."

"If only we could prove that."

"We must."

"Could Meeks have been at a party in Leonard's rooms, and then found his way back to the servants' quarters?"

"I very much doubt it. Not without being seen. He'd have to go down the landing, right past the cupboard where you and I were...well, hiding...down the main staircase, and through the passage that leads to the stairs."

"It's possible, isn't it?"

"But the place was crawling with hunters. We were the only ones they hadn't found. Besides Billie, there were Sir James and Lady Caroline, and Rex of course. Everyone hunting round the main part of the house, looking for us."

"But they're all in it together."

"I resent that remark, Mitch. Whatever is going on, Billie knows nothing about it, and if you don't believe me, I'll be extremely angry with you." His color was up; Morgan was extremely chivalric where ladies were concerned.

"Okay, okay, I believe you. I'm sure Belinda knows nothing. But Rex? Sir James and Lady Caroline?"

"Doesn't it strike you as odd, Mitch, that nobody found us for such a long time?"

"I wasn't really paying much attention to the game."

"No, I know what you were paying attention to. Corrupting your old pal Boy Morgan, who didn't know any better and who had been waiting for you to make a move since the first day he met you."

"Is that true?"

"Might be," he said, tousling my hair. I wanted to wrestle him to the floor and take him right there and then, but he kept me at arm's length. "Now just listen for a moment, Mitch. I've been thinking. That game of Sardines. It suited us, of course, for reasons that you well know, and it suited Billie, who's a big kid at heart. But I believe it suited everyone else in the house for very different reasons."

"You mean it got us out of the way."

"Precisely."

"While something was done in secret."

"Bingo. Everyone pretended to hide—but they were up to something."

"And when the police turned up, so soon after the discovery of the body..."

"Discovered by Belinda. I can't believe they would do something so awful to their own daughter. Stuffing a corpse in a cupboard where it would fall out on her."

"It was all planned. But why this weekend, with the house full of people?"

"That's what we have to find out, Mitch. Something happened. We don't know what. But something brought matters to a head."

"If only we knew what those 'matters' are."

"Well I can tell you something," Morgan said, with a satisfied grin. "Whatever it was, Sir James didn't like it."

"What do you mean?"

"While you were down the pub flirting with your secretary friend, don't tell me you weren't, I was making myself useful belowstairs."

"Not the fantastic tits again."

"The very same."

"And what did she have to reveal to you?"

"Nothing of that nature, though if I weren't such a decent chap I'd be tempted to sneak down there later on and give her what she wants. Why not join me, Mitch? Find out what you're missing."

"I'd rather you fucked me than her."

"Your loss. Think of both of us... Well, never mind. Anyway, she's a very naughty girl, our Susie. Very naughty indeed."

"I've heard about her loose morals from various quarters."

"You can't blame her for fucking Hibbert, can you? But

that's not what I meant. She's nosy. Inquisitive. Can't mind her own business."

"In other words, she saw something."

"She was on her way to a tryst with Hibbert when she heard Sir James and Lady Caroline arguing in the library. She stopped and listened, but couldn't make out what it was all about."

"Then?"

"They came bursting out of the library and chased each other up to Leonard's rooms. She watched them go in together and slam the door behind them."

"When was this?"

"Just about the time that you were getting my dick out of my trousers, I should think. She hid herself underneath the stairs and waited."

"So if Meeks had come down..."

"She would have seen him."

"And did she?"

"She never mentioned it. That's the trouble. Awkward for Meeks."

"But we know..."

"That's the trouble, Mitch. I'm not sure Burroughs was telling the truth."

"How come?"

"Because Susie said that Meeks was serving tea to the family in Leonard's rooms. She saw him go in—but she didn't see him come out. And he still hadn't come out when all hell broke loose."

"I refuse to believe Meeks is a murderer, or even an accomplice to murder. Now you have to believe me. It's all wrong."

"I believe you, then. I tell you what, though. She may not have seen Meeks coming out of Leonard's room, but she did see Sir James."

"What?"

"Yes. Storming out, he was, looking furious about something. Went off to his study and wasn't seen again until the police arrived."

"Maybe they found out what Leonard was up to with his friends."

"I don't believe he was up to anything of the sort. Not with Lady C in there as well. I think they were having some kind of meeting."

"But what about?"

"That's what we have to find out."

But where? We had looked in all the obvious places, even in a few of the less obvious ones, and all we were left with was suspicion and rumor. We left our room to "go hunting," as Morgan put it; we both knew that, if we stayed shut up together any longer, we'd let the trail go cold and spend the rest of the afternoon fucking. I could still feel the pleasure of his two long fingers up my ass, and was desperate to let him play the man with me. I was even prepared to "share" Susie, the kitchen maid, if it gave him pleasure. I knew it was time to get out and get my mind off sex.

We strolled along the network of landings on our floor, as if the truth was somehow going to pop out of a cupboard, like a partygoer in a game of Sardines—or, this being Drekeham Hall, like a corpse that's been planted in a covered-up murder.

"Boy," I said, suddenly stopping in my tracks. "What did Belinda see up here yesterday afternoon? Just before she found the body, I mean."

"Tracks on the carpet."

"Where were they leading from?"

"Sir James's study, she thought."

"That's where they were going to, though, isn't it? That's where they took the body. Look; if you rub the carpet toward us, as if you were dragging a body from the cupboard where it was found and into Sir James's study, the pile is just pressed flat. No tracks. This is where Belinda was standing, roughly, when she found the body. She wouldn't have seen anything."

I demonstrated with my foot, roughing up the pile in the appropriate direction.

"You're right."

"But if the body had been dragged in the other direction... Look." I rubbed my foot across the carpet the other way—in the direction that led from Leonard's rooms to the fatal cupboard. The pile, brushed up, made clearly visible tracks.

"So what Billie saw was not leading to Sir James's study," Morgan said, "but leading from Leonard's rooms..."

"And into the cupboard. Correct. So now we know where the murder took place."

"But that's exactly what Leonard told you."

"Yes. But he's lying about Meeks. Burroughs knew where Meeks was all afternoon. If we can prove that, and if we can make Leonard stick to his guns about the whereabouts of the murder, then we've got him."

"Do you think he killed Reg Walworth?"

"Not necessarily. But he knows who did."

"So it's all down to Burroughs. Poor old bastard. They'll turn him out when they know what he's been up to."

"And how easy it would be to discredit his evidence. Put the screws on someone like Hibbert, he'd blab. Then Burroughs is silenced, Mecks remains guilty on the evidence of the entire family, who will support Leonard's story, the scandal will be hushed up, Meeks hangs, Rex marries Diana... It's all very clever. Very neat."

"I say, Mitch, shut up a second." Morgan laid a hand on my arm.

"What?"

"Listen. Downstairs."

Voices were raised somewhere beneath us. We went

toward the source of the sound and lurked at the head of the stairs. There, at the front door, was the bulky form of Mrs. Ramage, giving short shrift to an unseen visitor.

"If you've come to sell something, we never buy at the door. Besides which, I would have thought that even someone of your class would have the common decency to come round the tradesman's entrance." She was quite gruff with anger.

"I'm not selling anything," came a man's voice. "I told you: I want to see Sir James."

"Do you have an appointment?"

"No, I don't."

"Then I suggest you make contact with our Mr. West on the telephone."

"I've come all the way from London..."

"It doesn't matter if you've come from Timbuktu, Mr...."

"Barrett. From the *London Evening News*."

"A journalist! Get away from here this instant before I call the police."

"I'm not breaking any laws, Missus." The voice had a slight cockney twang. "Just let me in."

"Certainly not. Speak to Mr. West. Good day." She slammed the door in the visitor's face and lumbered through the hall and out of sight.

"She's better than a bulldog," Morgan said.

What little I knew of the press I had gleaned from novels, but I got the impression that Mr. Barrett of the *London Evening News* conformed to the type, and wouldn't take no for an answer. If my reading was right, he would at this moment be sneaking around the side of the house and trying to find an alternative entrance that would circumvent the fearsome doorkeeper. I hastened out into the garden, cut through a shady alley that led from the drive, and—lo and behold!—met Mr. Barrett coming toward me. He was a man of roughly my height and build, that is to say, short and stocky, with a hat pushed back on his head, a cheap suit, and unpolished shoes. Little wonder Mrs. Ramage had given him such short shrift. I could see, however, that he had an inquisitive pugilist's face, with a broken nose, strong cheekbones, and a full, rubbery mouth. He was no oil painting, but I found him refreshing in these rarefied surroundings.

He was one step ahead of me.

"Afternoon, guv'nor. Just come about the guttering. Don't mind me. I know where I'm going."

"Glad to hear it, Mr. Barrett."

He didn't bother to keep up the pretense. "All right, all right. I'm on my way. Can't blame me for trying to do my job. God, this place has got tougher security than Buckingham Palace."

"Hold on," I said, steering him back toward the drive. "You and I need to have a little talk."

"What about?"

"We're interested in the same things, I guess."

"Oh, shit. You're not that Yank from the news agency, are you? The one that's scooping everyone else's stories? For God's sake, give a bloke a chance."

"No, I'm not a journalist. Come in here."

The garage, where Hibbert kept Sir James's Bentley, was open, and I pushed Barrett through. The air inside smelled not unpleasantly of petrol. Hibbert's cigarette ends were all over the floor. I wondered if this was where he brought Susie to keep her sweet.

"You want to see Sir James? Forget it."

"That's what his secretary said on the phone."

"Mr. West?"

"Yeah. Snotty little toerag."

"Sir James isn't seeing anyone. Least of all a journalist."

"Why not?"

"You tell me."

"Reg Walworth."

At last: the lead we'd been looking for. Someone who could shed light on the central mystery of the case—who, and what, was Reg Walworth, and why would anyone at Drekeham Hall want him dead?

"So who was he?"

"Who's asking?"

"Me? I'm just a friend of the family."

"How do I know that? You're a Yank. Yanks don't mix with the likes of Jimmy Eagle."

"I do."

"Don't believe you. You're a hack."

"I don't care if you believe me or not. You can go back to London for all I care. I'll just step indoors and have a word with Mrs. Ramage..."

"Oh, Christ, not her again. All right. Fair play. We'll work together if we have to, but don't you dare go running this as an exclusive..."

"I'm not a— Oh, forget it. I'll keep my information to myself. I'm way ahead of you already, Mr. Barrett, and I don't need help."

He looked at me with eyes used to making rapid calculations, and obviously figured that I had something to give him in exchange. He said, "I'll tell you who Reg Walworth is."

"And I'll tell you who the police are holding."

"What? They've got the killer already?"

"I didn't say that. But they're holding someone."

"This gets better and better. Looks like we've got plenty to share."

"You first."

"All right, Yankee boy. But for each piece of information I give you, you have to take off an article of clothing."

This was an unexpected turn. I'd seen calculation in those worldly little eyes, but nothing more. Still, it was a challenge.

"Fair enough. As long as you do the same."

"Looks like you're going to be naked first." He was right: I was still wearing my minimal summer wardrobe, whereas he was fully clothed. The prospect didn't displease me.

Barrett began. "Right. Reg Walworth. Shady character. Known by the police. Bit of form. Been done for soliciting."

"Come again?"

"Hold on there, pal. I think that counts as a piece of info, don't you?"

"Okay. Name it."

"Shoe."

I took off my left shoe.

"And he's done a bit of blackmailing as well, of a couple of old nobs that belong to the same club as Sir Jim. Other shoe, please."

I stood in my socks, which were soon filthy with engine oil and cigarette ash. I thought I'd better even up the score. "Just before Walworth's death, Sir James and Lady Caroline had a furious argument, and he stormed out of some kind of family meeting."

"Very generous of you, I'm sure," Barrett said. "Two items of information together."

"Hat and tie."

He obliged. "Want to get the jacket as well? I'm sure you can think of something."

"Oh, I've got plenty. The man they've arrested is the footman, Charlie Meeks. He's in Drekeham Police Station."

"Charlie Meeks? Never heard of him." Barrett peeled off his jacket, and hung it over the hood of the car. His shirt was a little less than perfectly white, and damp under the arms. He continued, "Right, my turn. Reg Walworth was invited down here by Sir James himself."

"I know that."

"You do?"

"He was coming down to discuss some improvements to the library wing."

"Who told you that?"

"His brother."

"That's worth a shoe or two." Barrett kicked off his shoes. "But how am I going to get you out of that shirt?"

"You'd better think of something, Mr. Barrett."

"Walworth had been visiting Sir James in his London flat..."

"He's a painter and decorator. It's not that unusual."

"He's nothing of the sort. He's a rent boy."

"What?"

"The shirt, please."

I pulled off my shirt, and couldn't resist flexing my muscles a little for his appreciation.

"Very nice, mate. Very nice." He stepped toward me, and the smell of fresh sweat mingled with the petrol and tobacco. "Your Sir James is a dark horse," he said, lowering his voice and taking my left nipple between finger and thumb. "Respectable family man, member of parliament, big noise in the business world, but behind the scenes, not all that he seems at all. He's got a lot to lose. The family is terrified of blackmail."

"And you think Reg Walworth—"

"The trousers."

I obeyed. Inside my underpants, I was fully stiff. All that remained were my socks, in which Barrett seemed uninterested; clearly, unlike some of my lovers, he was not queer for feet. He was, however, a tit man, and now had both of my nipples captive, tugging them and rolling them between finger and thumb.

"You've got some catching up to do, Yankee boy," he said, his mouth just inches from my ear. "Come on, give me some more."

In my eagerness to get Barrett naked, I racked my brain

for some concrete fact that would pass journalistic muster. "Sir James was involved in a political scandal last year that he hushed up at considerable personal expense. The family is broke."

"I thought as much," Barrett said, relinquishing my nipples so he could unbutton his shirt. "There have been rumors, of course, but nothing solid."

Solid was the right word: his body, which had appeared almost tubby in his badly cut suit, was a big slab of muscle. My eyes must have popped out of my head.

"Part-time bodybuilder. Health and strength and all that jazz," he said, striking a physique pose. "Like it?"

In answer, I grabbed his huge shoulders, bent down, and started sucking on his right tit. I've often found that, if a man pays a lot of attention to a particular part of your body, he wants you to do the same to him.

I was right. The moment he felt my mouth on his chest, he drew a huge breath and then groaned in ecstasy. Clamping my head down with one hand, he lifted me with the other arm around my waist and deposited me on the hood of the car. I had a feeling I was about to be pumped for information.

"And here's the clincher," he said. "Reg Walworth was threatening to communicate with Mortimer Hunt."

I managed to say "who?" through a mouthful of tit.

"Sir Mortimer Hunt, the Earl of Newington. Father of—"

"You win," I said, as the penny dropped and so did my pants. "Lady Diana Hunt. Rex's fiancée."

"Bingo," Barrett said, dropping to his knees. And that was the end of our information exchange. He swallowed my prick to the hilt and then, when I was wriggling around on the Bentley's shiny hood, thinking I was about to shoot my load, he lifted my legs and transferred his attention to my ass. He licked it till the hair was matted, then started probing in with his tongue. I had a pretty good idea what was to follow.

"Pity you didn't get my trousers down, Yankee boy," he said, unbuttoning himself and pulling out a prick that was as fat and thickset as the rest of him. "I'm going to have to fuck you like this."

"Go right ahead."

He grabbed my knees and shunted me forward—which was not pleasant, as my buttocks caught painfully on the shiny metal—and then, without ceremony, lined his dickhead up against my wet hole. Thank God he'd taken his time opening me up. He pushed into me as far as he could go, and I had to concentrate hard in order not to shout the place down, it hurt so much.

"Come on, mate, you can take it."

And I could. I breathed hard, waiting for my muscles to relax, while Barrett held my feet in his hands and rocked gently on his heels. He must have felt me loosening around him, because no sooner was I ready than he was pistoning into me.

"Fuck, that's good," he said, then spat down onto my cock to provide a bit of lubrication. "Let me see you wank yourself. I like seeing a bloke tossing himself off while I fuck him. Especially a nice muscular little number like you. Come on. Make yourself come."

I didn't need a second invitation, and as soon as I started jerking my cock the sensations up my ass were intensified by ten. I surrendered to the feeling and did nothing to prevent the orgasm that was hurtling toward me. After only a couple of minutes, I was thrashing around on the car. He knew exactly how to play me, and delivered the hardest, longest, roughest strokes that he could muster. He was rewarded by four copious wads of jizz that landed on my belly, my thighs, and the car's paintwork.

Barrett buried himself deep inside me, leaned forward as

far as he could, grabbed the back of my head, and kissed me on the mouth. And in that position he emptied his balls into my twitching hole.

X

AH, YOUTH! AT THE AGE OF TWENTY-TWO, MY POWERS OF recovery were prodigious. Perhaps this was due to the fact that I kept myself in good shape through sports; perhaps it was just the natural physical manifestation of my gargantuan sexual appetites. Whatever the reason, within an hour or so of being fucked silly on the hood of Sir James's Bentley, I was already looking forward to my next round with Morgan—or anybody else who might come along. My first taste of country house living was certainly giving me a lopsided view of the English upper classes.

With my balls drained and my asshole well fed, I felt calm enough to ponder the information imparted to me by Barrett in so singular a manner. Reg Walworth, our victim, was a prostitute who had been blackmailing Sir James, and who threatened Rex's marriage to Diana Hunt and thus the entire future of the Eagle family at Drekeham Hall. Sir James was queer, partially if not completely (he had, after all, fathered two children)—which explained the extraordinarily tolerant attitude toward sexual irregularity in his household. It also explained why he put up with so much from his odious younger brother, who, presumably, knew much and guessed more about his respectable sibling's private morals.

So at least I now had a motive for the crime; Reginald Walworth had met the fate of many a bungling blackmailer who overreached himself. But who had killed him? And why was Charlie Meeks being framed for the crime? Clearly his alleged guilt shifted suspicion from the Eagle family themselves—who, after all, were the only remaining suspects once Meeks was out of the picture. Leonard, Lady Caroline, Rex, and Sir James had been in the room on the afternoon Reg Walworth was murdered. Sir James had stormed out—disgusted by the crime, or refusing to assist? I could not believe he was the killer; this was a man of the highest professional and political probity. But who knew to what extremes a man would not go when his home was threatened? Rex, likewise, seemed an unlikely suspect—but he was hiding much, and could have played us all for a fool. Vince West had taught me that. That left Lady Caroline and her reptilian brother-in-law. She lacked the physical strength to throttle a man, but she might well desire his death. That left Leonard—strong, subtle, and, in moral terms, lower than worm's tits. And what of Leonard's shady "friends" from London—those bright young things and their rough-trade boyfriends whom, he alleged, he had been "entertaining" in his room? And what of Simon, the hall boy? What had he seen? What did he know? And how could he tell me?

In order to prove anything against the Eagle family, I first had to deal with the knotty problem of Charlie Meeks's whereabouts on the afternoon in question. He could not, after all, be in two places at one time, and I ruled out any suspicion of identical twins, the last resort of a detective writer in desperate need of a plot twist. How could he have served the family in Leonard's rooms, but gained his own quarters so soon, without passing through the main part of the house—where he would surely have been seen, either by Susie or by Belinda? If I could just find a way of moving that piece, the chess game would suddenly resolve itself.

I was sitting in the library, pondering all this in the aftermath of Barrett's thorough probing, when my attention was caught by the sound of crunching gravel and splashing water from the front drive. I wandered into the hall, peered through the Virginia creeper that hung in front of the windows, and saw Hibbert, the second footman, chauffeur, and general keeper of the cars, washing the very vehicle on which I had so recently been riding. He was wearing his chauffeur's uniform—gray trousers with a thick leather belt, black boots, a peaked cap—minus the jacket and minus the shirt. This was too interesting to be ignored, and I went out to investigate further.

Hibbert's reputation in the house was well established: he was a womanizer, a seducer of Mrs. Ramage's girls, the supposed husband-to-be of Susie, the kitchen maid, and a willing performer in Burroughs's stable of young male staff. Watching him washing the car, soaping it up with a bucket and sponge, I could see why. His body was built on classical lines, perfectly proportioned to his height—he was about 5' 9". He was dark in coloring, possibly of Asian extraction, and tanned even darker by his obvious love of the sun. He was hairy on the chest, stomach, and arms.

I wandered over to engage him in conversation; fortunately, I knew a bit about cars, and made some inane remark about Sir James's Bentley.

"Yes, sir, she's a beauty. Look at her chassis. She's a nice little goer, this one."

He had a cockney accent, and lacked the deference that most of the indoor staff showed. When he smiled, his handsome face broke up into dimples, and a small, crescent-shaped scar on his forehead was thrown into relief by the movement of his heavy black eyebrows. I suspected that he was a small-time crook engaged by Burroughs despite a colorful past and an equally eventful present. I understood how he could wrap Burroughs so neatly round his little finger. Well, if he was willing to perform for an old man like Burroughs, what might he not do for a virile young gentleman like me—and a guest, to boot? As you can see, I had fully recovered from my recent exertions.

I ran my hand over the fender. "Sleek as a racehorse, isn't she? And great suspension." To this I could testify, having given it a good workout earlier.

"Yeah," Hibbert said, washing down the exact spot where my ass had recently squirmed. "I like a nice easy ride myself."

"I bet you do."

"Can't stand it bumpy. I like to feel I'm on cushions, if you know what I mean."

I knew exactly what he meant—if he was fucking Susie, the kitchen maid, he must have a very comfortable ride indeed. I thought I would play along with this manly banter and see where it got me.

"Yeah—too many of your English girls are all skin and bone."

"You said it, mate. I like something I can get hold of." *Like your ass*, I thought, as he reached over toward the windshield. When he stood up, there were soap suds caught in his chest hair; he wiped them off absentmindedly with one brown hand.

"Me too. I've seen some nice, er, 'birds' here at Drekeham Hall."

"Not bad, some of 'em. Couple of nice tarts down in the kitchen, keep me busy enough."

"I bet they do." I'd keep him busy as well, especially with that little cap on his head.

"But I got bigger fish to fry."

"Oh, yeah?" I thought, like everyone else in Drekeham, he was about to turn into a raving homosexual before my very eyes. I was not averse to the idea. But Hibbert, alas, turned out to be the "look but don't touch" type.

"Yeah. A boy like me can go a long way if he knows how to play the game."

"And what game is that?"

"Hunt the Cunt." He grabbed his crotch and gave it a good squeeze.

"I'm sure you're very good at it."

"You bet I am. I'm the champion."

"And whose cunt have you hunted in Drekeham Hall?"

"I told you."

"What, the kitchen maid?"

"No, mate. You ain't listening. Hunt the Cunt." He winked and grabbed his crotch again, which seemed to be thickening up nicely.

"Wha—" And then I understood. Hunt the Cunt. Not a particularly nice nickname, but possibly a fitting one. I whistled.

"Wow, that's pretty good going."

"Yeah. She'll do."

"I bet."

"She's a fucking raver, mate. Can't get enough of it."

His packet was definitely bigger now; some men like nothing better than to brag about their sexual conquests. I was happy to listen. "Looks like you've got plenty to go around."

"I've had no complaints."

"So, you and Lady Diana Hunt. Who'd have thought it?"

"Well, she ain't getting much joy out of Rexy Boy, is she?"

"Isn't she?"

"Nah... He's a cold fish. More interested in business than

fuckin'. See, that's where I come in. Handy Hibbert. Always ready when called upon. And she calls upon me a lot."

"She likes that, does she?" I indicated his growing hard-on with my eyes. He stroked it, like a favorite dog.

"Can't get enough. Last night after dinner, again this morning, I've been fucking her in every possible position. She may be a Lady, but she ain't no lady, if you know what I mean."

I found his bragging extremely exciting, and longed to teach this arrogant little stud a lesson he would never forget.

"You must be exhausted."

"Nah. Don't worry about me. My tanks are always full. I mean, I spent half of yesterday screwing Fat Susie in her room, and I still had to have a wank when we got the afternoon off."

Watched by Burroughs, no doubt, I thought.

"Some afternoon off that turned out to be," he continued. "Oh, Mr. Hibbert, would you serve us tea? Oh, Mr. Hibbert, would you bring us sandwiches and whisky? Oh, Mr. Hibbert, would you assist Mr. Meeks with luncheon? They run me fuckin' ragged, mate." He took off his cap, wiped the sweat from his brow, and continued to wash the car. I watched with delight the play of muscles under his skin, but tried to concentrate on a niggling feeling somewhere at the back of my mind that, for once, wasn't lust.

"So you were working too, then, when you were supposed to have a half day?"

"Yeah. Bloody liberty I call it. Typical of this family."

"What were you doing?"

"Looking after the little party in Mr. Leonard's room."

"With Charlie Meeks?"

"Yeah. What of it?"

"Nothing. Just can't believe how these English families think they can get away with abusing their staff like that."

"Don't worry about me, mate." He smiled again, and it was like the sun breaking out on a cloudy day. "I'm taking them for the ride of their life."

"How so?"

"Went up there with Meeks, did our bit, kowtowing to all that lot, serving everything up nice, then when nobody was looking I nipped down to see my little Susie in the servants' quarters."

"That was brave, considering the house was overrun at the time."

"Ah!" He tapped the side of his nose. "That's where the back passage comes in handy, mate."

"The back passage?"

"Yeah, and not the one you're thinking about." He winked; just how well had he interpreted my appraisal of his body?

"Which one, then?"

"There's a corridor runs along the back of the family's rooms on the first floor, all the way along to the staircase that joins the staff's quarters. Funny little rat run, can't imagine what it was built for. But it's done me a few good turns."

"You mean it can be accessed from Leonard's room?"

"Yeah, from Leonard's room, from Rex's room, from Sir James's study, from the blue room where you're sleeping, from the rose room where Lady Diana is...well, not sleeping much, as it turns out. Yeah, I'm up and down that passage like a yo-yo."

"Who else knows about it?"

"A few of us."

"You mean there's a secret passage that connects the staff quarters to the family's bedrooms and nobody's done anything to have it closed off?"

"Why should they? It's the name of the game in this house. Upstairs, downstairs, they're all fuckin' like rabbits, the lot of 'em. Ask Mr. Burroughs."

"I have spoken to Mr. Burroughs."

"Oh, yeah?" He grinned again. "Expect he told you a bit about me, did he?"

"He did."

"He's a dirty old fucker, that one. Still, I don't mind. I can keep him sweet"—he squeezed his cock again—"and he keeps me out of trouble. Fair exchange, I call it."

"Sounds like a good deal to me."

"Which side's your bread buttered on, then, mate? You one of them and all?"

"Yep."

"Thought so when I picked you up at the station. What about your mate, Miss Belinda's bloke?"

This was going too far. "He's Miss Belinda's bloke."

"No offense. Just wondered. You sharing a room and that—"

"Have you been spying?"

"Me? No. Doesn't interest me. Don't get me wrong: sex is sex, it's all good. But it just happens that I've got enough pussy on my hands at the moment, I don't need anything else. And I'm not one of them that gets off on watching other people at it. There's plenty here that do."

"So I gather."

"But not me. I like to show it, not watch it."

"Good job."

"You want a quick flash?"

"Go ahead. See what all the fuss is about."

"Okay. Hold this." He gave me his bucket and positioned himself beside the driver's door so that he could not be seen from the house or the gate.

"Here you are." He flopped out a cock that was even darker than the rest of him and was half-hard.

"Nice."

"Gets bigger, watch."

He stood with his hands on his hips and started swaying

gently. With each movement, his dick climbed five degrees. It reached the horizontal, then continued until it was pointing skyward. At its full extent, it just cleared the top of his thick leather belt.

"Now I can see why you're so much in demand around here."

"Too right," he said. "I'd let you suck it, but I've got to save it for those that pay for it."

"Lady Diana."

"Yeah. She'll be ringing for her pre-dinner fuck soon. Can't disappoint a lady, can I?"

"God forbid."

"You can have a quick taste, if you want. I don't mind."

I needed no second invitation, and dropped to my knees to give it a suck. The sound of the front door of Drekeham Hall opening brought me to my senses.

"Mitch!" Morgan's voice.

"Coming!"

I stood up, and Hibbert stuffed his prick back into his trousers.

"Nice one, mate," he said. "Got it wet for me. I'll come and fuck you later, if you like."

"Why? Pussy not enough for you?"

"You've got a pussy, ain't you?"

"Maybe."

"I fancy going to America."

"I see."

"Bet you're rich. All you Yanks are rich."

"Not rich enough to afford you, Hibbert."

"Oh, well. Can't blame me for trying. If you change your mind..."

The arrogant little bastard! I could have wrestled him to the ground and fucked him then and there. But there were more pressing concerns.

"Mitch! Where the hell are you?"

"I'm here!"

I ran back to the house, leaving Hibbert cleaning the car and whistling through his teeth.

Morgan looked flustered. "For God's sake, Mitch, where do you keep disappearing to? I've been looking for you for the last hour."

I didn't feel I could tell him the whole truth, and contented myself with half. "I've been conducting interviews."

"Yes, well, so have I—with Simon, the hall boy."

"You spoke to him?"

"Certainly I did."

"And what did he say?"

"He said nothing, of course. Poor lad can't form a word, just a lot of noises that don't add up to anything. But God, he tried so hard to make himself understood. He was straining so hard, I was scared we were going to be overheard, so I took him into our room."

"And what happened there?" I had a twinge of jealousy—whether it was over Morgan, whom I thought of as "mine," or over Simon, whom I had been interested in fucking ever since I laid eyes on him, I'm not sure.

"I sat him down in a chair and got him to calm down, gave him a glass of water. He was in a terrible state. Kept showing me those marks on his wrists."

"Ah—the rope burns."

"Well, that's what I thought they were, until I took a closer look at them. They weren't burns, really; I've had rope burns from mucking about in tree camps as a kid, I know what they look like. These were more like something hard had cut into his flesh. Very nasty."

"You don't think he'd tried to...kill himself?"

"Christ, no, Mitch, don't be so dramatic. But I knew something bad had happened to him, and so I did something rather brilliant."

"What?"

"I gave him a piece of paper and a pencil, of course."

"Oh. Is that all?"

"Perhaps you're not interested in what he wrote, then?"

"Okay, okay. You're a genius. Just tell me."

"Well, I wrote down questions and he wrote down the answers, as best he could. I don't think he got much of an education, poor lad, and he labored over every letter, sticking his tongue out, he was concentrating so hard."

"What did you ask him?"

"First of all, I asked him what had happened to his hands. I had to do a lot of dumb show to explain what I'd written. This is what he wrote in reply." Morgan handed me a piece of paper on which some badly formed letters spelled out H-A-N-C-U-F-S.

"Handcuffs?"

"Exactly. Then I asked who did it to him, and he wrote P-L-I-C-E-M-A-N."

"Policeman. Oh, God."

"When I asked him if he knew his name, he shook his head. So I asked him where he had been handcuffed. Look what he wrote."

K-I-T-C-H-I-N.

"The kitchen? But Leonard said they'd had him tied up on his bed during some kind of orgy."

"Exactly. So that's another piece of Leonard's story that doesn't add up. Then I asked him when it had happened, and he wrote Y-E-S-T-Y. I think that must mean yesterday; I always had a bit of trouble spelling that word myself."

"So, yesterday afternoon, while Leonard was supposedly entertaining in his rooms, the cops handcuffed Simon in the kitchen...to keep him out of the way?"

"I'm sure of it. Then I made the poor kid blush terribly. I asked him if anyone had done anything to him. I thought he was going to start crying, he was so embarrassed."

"What did he write?"

"He didn't write anything. He just pointed to his bum."

"My God, you don't think they..."

"No. I asked him what they'd done, and he dropped his trousers and showed me. I must say, he's got a very nice little bum, very smooth and hard."

"Spare me the descriptions, Morgan. What did you see?"

"Stripes. He'd been whipped."

"Why? What for?"

"That's what I asked him. And he wrote this."

In confused letters, the words S-A-Y N-O.

"Say no? What does he mean? Say nothing? Don't tell anyone?"

"No," Morgan said. I think it means he said no to whatever the police tried to get him to do. Your guess is as good as mine."

"A good deal better, if what I saw earlier on in the police station is anything to go by. He's a very brave kid."

"Then he wrote B-E-L-L R-I-N-G and P-L-I-C-E-M-A-N G-O-N. So he was left alone down there until someone came and let him go, with his trousers round his ankle and his poor bare bum covered in painful red weals. I felt so sorry for him."

"What did you do?"

"I took him into our bathroom and cleaned his bum with a bit of disinfectant, which must have stung like hell, but at least it won't scar. Then I rubbed a bit of ointment on it, that posh stuff that you use on your hands."

"Oh, did you indeed."

"Hmmm... He wouldn't stand up straight when I'd finished, he was trying to hide something with his hands. I reassured him as best I could, so he relaxed and got dressed. He gave me such a big hug when he left. I slipped him a couple of bob."

"You mean you didn't...?"

"No I did not! I'm not one to take advantage of a young man like that. Shame on you, Mitch."

"I just wondered."

"So anyway, if you can bring your one-track mind back to what really matters, it looks like we have a potential witness who's been got out of the way, and another big black mark against the family."

"And the police."

"Exactly."

"But they were careless. They thought that just because Simon can't speak and can't hear, he wouldn't tell. They just mistreated him and let him go. Very foolish."

"And very cruel," Morgan said, obviously more smitten with Simon than he was letting on. I'd have to watch him.

"I get the feeling that things are reaching some kind of denouement," I said.

"De-what?"

"Things are coming to a climax."

"Not again."

"We have to go on a little adventure, Morgan. Follow me."

"Where are we going?"

"To bed."

"Hoped we might be!"

"But this time, we're not going to fuck."

"Oh. Damn. Been wanting to all day."

"Patience, young man. Patience will be rewarded."

"With your arse, I hope."

I didn't mention that my ass needed a little time to recover.

We strolled upstairs, trying to look nonchalant, when Mrs. Ramage appeared out of nowhere and blocked our way.

"Aren't you two young gentlemen outside?"

"Apparently not, Mrs. Ramage," I said.

"On a lovely day like today. The hunt will be passing through shortly. You really ought to see it. The Drekeham Hunt is the finest in the country."

"So I gather."

"Doesn't Sir James ride today, Mrs. R?" Morgan asked, much better at this kind of bluff, meaningless conversation than me.

"Sir James is under the weather, sir," the hefty housekeeper said, pursing her lips. "Lady Caroline has advised him to keep indoors today. Such a shame."

"Well, we'll be sure not to miss the hunt. What time do they come round, Mrs. R?"

"About four, sir."

"Marvelous. Just time to go and freshen up."

"Were you going to your room, sir?"

"Yes, Mrs. R. Just for a sec."

"We were...about to clean it, that's all."

She was walking backward, as if she wanted to bar our door.

"That's all right, we won't be a tick," Morgan said. "Mr. Mitchell's been playing, er—tennis, was it, Mitch?"

"That's right. Just hitting some balls back and forth."

"I didn't see you, sir."

"And he needs to change his shirt. You know how fussy these Americans are. We'll be down in a jiffy, then your marvelous girls can come and work their magic on our bachelor quarters."

Mrs. Ramage was seized with a fit of coughing, which obliged her to bend double in our doorway, making it quite impassible. Morgan patted her on the back, and gently maneuvered her to one side.

"You want to take something for that chest, Mrs. R," he said, winking at me. "Sounds like it could turn nasty."

Mrs. Ramage bustled off down the landing, leaving us—finally—to ourselves.

The moment I walked into the room, I could see that something was wrong. My books were not as I had left them, neatly piled on the desk; they were spread out, some of them on the floor, others on the bed. My suitcase, which had been messy but at least contained, now looked as if it had exploded.

"I say, someone's been looking through my shaving kit," Morgan said from the bathroom. "How odd."

"Not odd at all," I said. "We've had uninvited guests."

"Where are you?" Boy said, viciously pulling back curtains and opening cupboard doors.

"They're gone, whoever they were," I said. "And I know exactly where."

The window was closed, the catch locked from the inside. Morgan looked perplexed.

"Try that door over there," I said, pointing to what I had hitherto assumed was the maid's cupboard—a half-height door in the back wall, papered over with the same blue floral wallpaper as the rest of the room.

"Don't be daft, Mitch. That's where they keep the linen." He went up to the door, crouched down, and jokingly shouted "Halloooo! Come out, come out, wherever you are!"

"See?" he said. "There's nothing..."

And then, coming from several feet further along the wall, there was a dull thud.

"What the—"

"Shh! Listen!"

Floorboards squeaked somewhere—on the landing? And then there was silence.

"This door, I think you will find, opens the way to our mystery."

"You've been reading too much," Morgan said.

"Try it."

He scrabbled at the edge of the little door with his fingers; there was no knob. "Locked."

"Quite. From the other side."

"Must be."

Mrs. Ramage's voice croaked from the landing. "Mr. Morgan! Mr. Mitchell! Are you decent?"

"Just a minute, Mrs. R! Mitchell's on the pot!" Morgan stifled a snicker. "That should put her off for a bit."

"We've got to get this door open," I whispered, "and quietly, or we'll have Mrs. Ramage and all the rest of them down on us."

"Leave it to Boy." To my astonishment he picked up a paper knife from the desk, ran it dexterously round the edges of the door, and then, when it met with an obstruction, wriggled and wiggled it until there was a pop and a click. The door swung open.

"The back passage..."

Morgan was ahead of me, already half through the door on his hands and knees. I could hear the heavy footfall of Mrs. Ramage in the corridor outside our room, so I pushed him through and followed. We closed the door behind us and replaced the catch that Morgan had managed to lever open. Then we crouched in the darkness, waiting for our eyes to adjust.

I did not imagine for one moment that Mrs. Ramage, a housekeeper in an English country house, would ever dream of invading the privacy of a guest's room—but something urgent was pressing her. We heard the bedroom door open.

"Mr. Morgan? Mr. Mitchell? Are you in the bathroom?"

We hardly breathed. Mrs. Ramage walked across the bedroom and knocked on the bathroom door.

"Gentlemen? Are you in here? It's Mrs.— Oh, my God!"

Then her heavy steps ran back from the bathroom—which she had, of course, found empty—and out onto the landing. We heard her pounding away, though it was impossible to tell in which direction. She knew exactly where we had gone—but was unable to follow us, being a) far too large to get through the little door and b) unable to open it from the bedroom side.

I lit a match. The passage extended for yards on either side of us—the whole length of the house, by the look of it. It was about four feet high, with a ceiling that sloped down toward the outer wall; clearly this cavity had been built inside the thick walls in a way that would never excite suspicion from the outside. Perhaps it was a remnant of the Civil War? An escape route for recusant Catholics? I had heard of such things. Whatever its original purpose, it was now the perfect conduit to illicit sexual relations between family and staff.

The match burned out, and once our eyes had adjusted to the gloom we could just make out the faint outline of other doors further along the passage in each direction. So this was how Hibbert played his little game of Hunt the Cunt—and, more important, this was how Charlie Meeks could have been in two places at one time. There, a few yards down the passage, was the door that led to Leonard Eagle's rooms. And this way...

"Come on, Mitch," whispered Morgan. "We'll have to crawl."

I didn't object; crawling along the passage meant that I had my nose up his butt. At one point he stopped, and my entire face was buried between his cheeks; just the place I liked it to be.

He held up a hand; I could just see it in the gloom. There were voices from nearby.

"I'm sorry, sir, but I couldn't very well stop them."

"For God's sake, Ramage, what did I tell you?" It was Sir James—and he was furious.

"What do you expect me to do? This whole situation is ridiculous, and you know it."

I could not believe that Mrs. Ramage would speak to her employer in this way.

"And now, thanks to you, they've found their way into... Oh, my God."

There was an almighty thud on the wall by our heads as Sir James, presumably, attacked the door from his study, outside which we had parked ourselves. Morgan was swift to act; half crouching, half crawling, he loped along the rest of the passageway without a sound. I did my best to follow, but I crashed into the wall every five feet or so, giving a perfect indication of our progress. From the other end of the passage, I heard a bell ring; someone was summoning assistance, and our escape would soon be blocked.

Morgan stopped a few yards along, and was muttering to himself. "Five, six, seven, that's you and me, Whopper, Sir James...then we must be over the garage and into the servants' quarters. Hello, what's this, then?"

There was another door, quite unlike the other low openings; this one was full-sized.

"I wonder what's..."

A click and a thud behind us; someone had come into the passage from Sir James's room.

"Quick, Mitch," Morgan said, with his hand on the doorknob. "This way." It opened without a sound, and we closed it as silently as we could, finding ourselves in what appeared to be a lumber room above the garage. There was a light switch on the wall—but to use it would have been to betray our position for certain. Morgan braced himself against the door—thank God for those strong rower's muscles!—and I cast around for a means of escape.

A faint illumination came in through a filthy, overgrown skylight in the roof—and I could see that, far from being a lumber room, this strange little attic was fitted out as a photographic darkroom with a sink, bottles of chemicals, and a rudimentary old enlarger of the bellows variety. Strips of negatives hung from pegs like washing on a line. I longed to look at them—but suddenly there was a battering on the door.

"Can't hold them for long!" Morgan said. "Open that window!"

"We'll break our necks."

"Do it!"

I jumped up onto the work surface behind the sink, and nearly slipped on something small and cylindrical under my foot—a roll of film. Not knowing what to do with it, I put it into my pants pocket.

The skylight was crucial inches too high for me, and I couldn't reach the catch.

Morgan wedged a chair against the door and leaped up beside me.

"Here, let me. Hold the door."

I did what I could—but I was too late. The door was breaking open just as Morgan pushed the skylight open and was rewarded with a face full of debris. I was pitched onto the floor.

"Mitch!"

"Go, Boy! Go now! I'll follow."

He disappeared through the skylight, and I picked myself up.

There was a small metallic click, and the room was flooded with light.

"Not so fast, Mr. Mitchell."

The doorway was blocked by the unmistakable form of Mrs. Ramage.

I jumped up onto the counter and grabbed the frame of the skylight; Morgan's hand reached down to pull me up.

"Stop right there, or you're dead."

She stepped back, and there behind her was Sergeant Kennington. And he was holding a gun.

XI

I WAS FROG-MARCHED ALONG THE REST OF THE BACK passage by Sergeant Kennington, who twisted my arm and seemed to take pleasure in my yelps of pain. Pushed down the spiral stone stairs at the end, I nearly fell; it would have suited their purposes, perhaps, if I had broken my neck. In seconds I was in Mrs. Ramage's office, a square, gloomy room with a single high window in the outer wall. Kennington pushed me into a chair and, forcing my hands back through the frame, handcuffed me in position. Whatever Simon, the hall boy, had escaped, I was about to make up for.

"Where is it, Mr. Mitchell?" Mrs. Ramage said, in a voice that could have curdled milk in the kitchen next door.

"Where's what?" I thought it better to feign ignorance, though I had a good idea what she was talking about—the roll of film that I had picked up in the darkroom. While Kennington had pinned me against the wall upon my "arrest," Mrs. R had been furiously casting around for something, and could not find it.

"You know what I mean. Search him, Kennington."

The handsome, cold-eyed policeman grinned wolfishly and started feeling around in my pockets. Fortunately, I had taken the opportunity while we were tussling in the darkroom to slip the roll of film into a secret compartment, namely, my asshole. It had hurt, as it was both an awkward shape and unlubricated, but that's never stopped me before. Now all I had to do was keep Kennington from looking up there.

Kennington lacked the gentle touch, and I well knew that he had a sadistic streak. He pushed and pulled me so that the handcuffs cut into my knuckles; when searching my shirt pocket, he pinched and twisted my tits. In order to feel around in my pants, he pushed his forearm against my windpipe and forced my head back, tilting the chair while rummaging around my nether regions. Fighting for breath, I kicked him in the shins.

"That was stupid, sir," he said, with oozing sarcasm. "Can't have you assaulting a police officer." And so he grabbed a couple of hand towels that were hanging on Mrs. Ramage's dresser and proceeded to tie my ankles to the chair legs.

"It would make life so much easier if you would just give us what we want," Mrs. Ramage said, her face a mask of hostility.

"I haven't got anything you want," I said, struggling with Kennington's brutal investigation of my pants.

"We'll see about that," he said, squeezing my balls unpleasantly hard. Much as this hurt, it suddenly gave me hope. I remembered from Kennington's conversation with Piggott in the police station that he had availed himself of his subordinate's huge, clublike prick; perhaps I could count on the sergeant's hungry ass to keep him well away from mine. As long as he could be distracted by my prick, then my hidden treasure might remain inviolate.

"You're being very foolish, Mr. Mitchell," Mrs. Ramage said. "You don't imagine, do you, that your position as a guest in this house would protect you? Not after all that's happened."

"Nothing would surprise me in Drekeham Hall, Mrs. Ramage."

"Nobody knows where you are. Nobody will come looking for you."

Right on cue, a voice from the outside world penetrated the window. It was distant, possibly on the other side of the house—but it was perfectly audible.

"Mitch! Where are you? Mitch!"

It was Morgan, of course, who I knew would be running around the grounds like an excited retriever, trying to find me.

I drew breath to reply, but was immediately cut off by Kennington's hand over my mouth and nose.

"If you make so much as a peep, Mr. Mitchell," Mrs. Ramage said, "Kennington here will quite happily throttle you."

She wasn't kidding; Kennington held his huge hand over my face, preventing me from breathing, while he continued to squeeze my nuts. This was obviously his idea of fun, and while I'm not averse to a little friendly bondage, this was out of my league.

"You've been nothing but trouble since you arrived," Mrs. Ramage said, watching me turning purple. "Perhaps it would be best to just get you out of the way right now. What do you think, Kennington?"

"Let me take care of him, Mrs. R."

"Very well. I leave you in Sergeant Kennington's capable hands. How stupid of you to try and interfere in what doesn't concern you."

I was really struggling now, desperate to draw air. Just as I started feeling faint, Kennington removed his hand, laughing like a cruel boy torturing a puppy. I coughed and choked, but I could breathe again.

"You won't get away with this," I said. "Morgan will find me."

"Oh, your precious bloody Morgan. He's easily managed. Leave that to Sir James. He will have found him by now and he'll soon send him packing. No, Mr. Mitchell, I'm afraid your friend will be of little use to you now. You're on your own."

"Perhaps you'd like to join Meeks in the cells," Kennington said, leering in my face. "You saw how well we treated him, didn't you? Dirty little spy. We don't like spies, do we, Mrs. R?"

"And we don't like stupid young men who get ideas above their station and rock the boat. But with you and Meeks out of the way, Drekeham Hall can run smoothly again. Sir James has learned his lesson. Things are going to change round here again. I'll see to that. Law and order will be restored. Thank goodness we can rely on the police."

"You know you can do that, Mrs. R."

"I should bloody well hope so, too, Kennington, the amount Sir James has paid you to sort this out."

So Sir James was behind the arrest of Charlie Meeks—but I still didn't understand why it was the footman who was being framed for the crime.

Mrs. Ramage was working herself into a fury; her face, twisted with emotion, was haggard and even uglier than usual.

"Why did you want to go sticking your nose in? We sort things out our own way in this country."

"By murder?"

"Murder? What do you know about murder?"

"It's a crime. You'll hang for it."

"Don't worry about my neck, Mr. Mitchell," Mrs. Ramage said, fondling her wattles. "The only one that's going to get stretched belongs to Charlie Meeks. Good riddance to bad rubbish. He's been nothing but trouble in this house since he arrived, breaking the rules, flouting traditions—"

The electric bell above Mrs. Ramage's door rang, hard and sudden. We all jumped.

"Let them get their own bloody tea for once," she muttered. "Where's that film, Kennington? Haven't you found it?"

"He hasn't got it."

"Morgan has it," I lied.

"Don't lie to me!" Mrs. Ramage screamed in my face. "Or you'll—"

The bell rang again, longer this time.

"For God's sake!" she said, showering my face in saliva. "I told them not to disturb me."

"It's coming from Leonard's room," Kennington said, checking the panel of lights above the door.

"I've had enough trouble from that quarter to last me a lifetime," Mrs. Ramage said.

"Perhaps he wants someone else killed," I said. This was foolish: Mrs. Ramage drew herself up to her full height and put her not inconsiderable weight behind a punch that connected with my jaw and knocked the chair over, with me strapped into it. I feared that she was going to follow up with a few kicks from her large booted feet, but before she could strike, the door burst open and there stood Leonard Eagle himself, out of breath and evidently shaken. He must have raced down the back passage.

"Damn it, Ramage, didn't you hear me ringing?"

"Can't you see I'm busy?"

"You'd better come upstairs right now. It's Burroughs."

The effect on Mrs. Ramage was electric; she literally jumped backward. "What? What's happened?"

"He's hanged himself."

She screamed, tottered, and nearly fell on top of me;

Kennington held her arm, thank God, or I might not be here to tell the tale.

"Where is he?"

"He's in my room. We cut him down just in time."

"I'm coming, Wilfred!" screamed Mrs. Ramage, running out of the door like a maenad. We heard her lumbering up the stairs, alternately screaming and whimpering. Leonard followed her on catlike feet.

Before I had time to ponder this extraordinary turn of events, Kennington roughly righted the chair and grabbed me by the chin.

"Now I've got you all to myself," he said. "No witnesses. No intruders."

"Do your worst."

"I intend to."

He bolted the door and started unbuttoning his tunic. "No point in getting my uniform dirty. Bloodstains show, even on dark-blue cloth."

"I'm not afraid of you."

"Well, you should be."

He dropped his tunic on a chair, pulled down his braces, and started unbuttoning his shirt. His body was wiry like a lightweight boxer's; I had already found out how strong he was.

Taking advantage of my immobility, he sat astride my thighs, grabbed the back of my head, and squashed my face against his chest. It smelled sweaty. I was pressed into the hair beneath his pectoral muscles so hard that I couldn't even open my mouth; my nose was crushed sideways. Obviously PC Kennington was queer for asphyxiation; I would have to distract him.

"We've got all evening to play with," he said. "No one's going to disturb us. They're busy upstairs. So what shall I do first?"

Pressing my face even harder into his chest, he started

bucking his hips, rocking the chair—and I could feel that he was hard, as his groin pressed into my stomach. Power—and the abuse of power—turned him on. Whatever he had planned, I had to distract him and get the game back onto my own terms. Seldom have I started my conquest of a man from such a disadvantage.

I guessed that, if I could give the impression that I was enjoying this rough treatment, I might be able to excite Kennington's sexual appetite, and quell his sadism. I don't mind rough handling, but I have no desire for pain, and certainly not for death at the hands of a deranged assassin.

I managed to open my jaw just enough to slip my tongue between my teeth and started mashing it against Kennington's chest. The effect was instant.

"Oh—" he gasped, as if it was the last thing on earth he expected to feel. "I see. Like that, do you?"

I wasn't sure whether he sounded excited or disappointed—but at least he backed off enough to allow me to open my mouth, breathe easily through my nose, and continue licking his chest with greater freedom. I found his left tit and paid some attention to that, and the hand on the back of my head began to caress rather than push. After that nipple was so erect that I could easily have bitten it off, he guided my head over to the other. The moment my tongue touched his right tit, he twitched like a lunatic. It is often the case, I have found, that while one tit gives a man pleasure, the other is a trigger for ecstasy. Kennington was a right-tit man.

"You fucking queers," he said, watching my tongue and lips playing with his nipple. "You're all the same. You love it, don't you?" I have heard this kind of crap before from "straight" men who can only enjoy gay sex if it's spiced with abuse; I wasn't about to argue, as it seemed to be leading Kennington exactly where I wanted him to go. I looked up at him, licked my lips, and let my mouth hang open. It couldn't have worked better; he stood up, unbuttoned his fly, and pulled out his hard prick. It was a handsome tool, with a particularly large helmet, fully exposed and already sticky.

My instinct was to lunge, but it was important to give Kennington the impression that he was still in control—so I just sat there and allowed him to "force" me. Thankfully, I've had a lot of practice at cocksucking, and knew how to keep breathing when he stuck the whole length of his dick into my mouth. He started fucking my throat—and, every time he pulled back sufficiently, I grabbed a breath through my nostrils. My eyes, however, were watering—and this he liked, as he made a point of wiping away the tears and tasting them. If I could make him come, would he let me go? I didn't know what to expect—but at least while he was fucking my mouth, he wasn't killing me—and he was steering clear of my ass, where something was hidden that, for reasons I didn't yet know, he wanted to get his hands on.

It suddenly occurred to me that if he continued to fuck my mouth like this, he might get the urge to fuck my ass, and this would be disastrous for me. I had no desire to have a hard-edged roll of film pushed up into my lower intestine—nor did I want him to find the evidence. How could I divert his train of thought?

I remembered his conversation with Piggott and his rueful but pleasant memory of being fucked, so I decided that, if I could just hit his anal switch, I might save myself. The moment he pulled out of my mouth and started jerking off in my face, I dived for his balls, then down to his perineum—and this did the trick. Thinking that he was adding to my humiliation, and to his power over me, Kennington made his big mistake. He turned around, dropped his pants around his ankles, spread his cheeks, and stuck his ass in my face.

"Go on then, if you're so keen, lick that!"

Feigning a decent amount of distaste (but noticing with relief that he was scrupulously clean in that area), I waited for him to back into me. As soon as his parted buttocks made contact with my face, I got to work with my tongue. I licked his firm, dark-pink hole, lapping at it like a dog lapping at a bowl of water. This had the desired effect; Kennington moaned, spread his cheeks even further, and pressed into me. This enabled me, by dint of bracing my feet firmly against the floor, to penetrate him with my tongue.

And, as I expected, the mood suddenly changed. Kennington was exactly what I thought he was—essentially passive, at least in the anal area. He may have enjoyed abusing my mouth for the illusion of power it gave him, but what his body really wanted was to be penetrated. His ass opened up like a flower, and I managed to get an inch of tongue into him.

This continued for a few minutes, until my tongue, lips, and jaw were screaming in agony—but it was enough. He stood up with his trousers still around his ankles—they were too narrow to pull over his stout police boots, and he was in a hurry—and undid my fly. He yanked my pants halfway down my thighs, and my cock bounced free. Thank God I've always managed to respond physically to any kind of stimulus, however strange the circumstances; it was vital at this point that Kennington could get exactly what he wanted.

When he saw my hard prick bouncing around on my stomach, he drew in his breath, muttered "Oh, fuck, yes," and spat into his hand. He slathered my prick up, turned around again and started reversing onto me. I had to raise my ass from the seat so that my hips were sticking out; this put a terrible strain on my back and thighs, but I was young and strong and desperate. Kennington grabbed my prick, steered it into himself, and then sank onto it. The ring of his sphincter was tight, and I felt sure I must be hurting him—but inside he was as soft as silk. I managed to buck my hips a few times, but there was not enough leverage to get a really good fuck going.

Kennington realized this, and dragged the chair so that my back was against the wall—somehow keeping my prick inside him all the time—then braced himself against a dresser and pushed backward. In this position, I was able to fuck him as hard as he could possibly have desired, and I must confess with a certain amount of embarrassment that the restraints on my hands and wrists added considerably to my excitement. Kennington's butt, of which I had a perfect view, was lean and muscular, deeply indented on the side of each buttock, and I could see his gluteal muscles working to extract the most pleasure from each stroke.

This could not go on for long, and I could feel an orgasm rising within me. The sensations were considerably heightened by the fact that my ass was contracting around the hard edges of the film canister. I prayed that I wouldn't eject it at the crucial moment.

Kennington was oblivious to everything, his head thrown back, his cock pumping his fist, and a stream of obscenities pouring from his lips. Sweat was running down his back, and I tasted it with my tongue; this was all he needed to send him over the edge, and with a roar he started squirting spunk all over the dresser, into the teacups, over Mrs. Ramage's household accounts.

I wasn't far behind him, but I knew I must act quickly. And so, with one almighty thrust, I managed to lever the still twitching Kennington further over the edge of the dresser and get myself into a semistanding position—as much as the ties at my ankles and wrists would allow. And then, as I started to come inside him, I grabbed the edge of the dresser and smashed myself rapidly backward against the wall. My cock flew out of Kennington's ass, and he dropped to his knees as limp as a rag doll while the next three spurts of spunk flew all over his back. The chair, which was a reasonably sturdy wooden construction, creaked noisily, and then, with another terrible smash that took the skin off my knuckles, it shattered. A couple more bashes were enough to reduce it to firewood.

My hands were still attached behind my back, and I could not break the frame of wood that held them shackled—but my legs were free, though there were still bits of wood tied to them. Just as Kennington turned to get up, I kicked him with all my might in the stomach, knocking his wind out completely. Another swift kick brought his head into contact with the edge of the dresser; he fell and knocked himself out cold on the floor.

With Kennington out of action, I managed to smash what remained of the chair, locate his keys, and undo the handcuffs after a lot of twisting and fiddling and cursing. My cock was still dripping with come, and I took advantage of the unconscious Kennington's upturned face to wipe the last few drops off against his parted lips. I thought he would have liked that.

I pulled up my trousers, unbolted the door, and ran like hell.

XII

My head still spinning from the violent events of the last hour, I raced up the stone steps and regained the back passage. How many more times would I have to thrust my way up and down that dark, dank tunnel before my weekend at Drekeham Hall was over?

I didn't have to go all the way this time; my target was Leonard Eagle's chambers. I passed by the darkroom, and saw that it had been completely wrecked; the enlarger lay smashed on the floor, the drawers were all pulled open, their contents spread on the floor, the negatives in tatters on every surface.

The half-height door that led to Leonard's room was open, so I made not a sound as I approached it on all fours. Fate was on my side; there was a hubbub of voices from the other side, and the last thing they were expecting was any kind of attack from the rear. Crouching in the semidarkness and peeping through the crack between door and frame, all I had to do was watch and listen as the final act of the drama was played out in front of me.

A group of figures stood with their backs toward me: I recognized Sir James, Lady Caroline, Leonard, and Lady Diana, all of them talking at once. Above their voices I heard a strange, low mooing sound like a stricken heifer.

"For God's sake, Ramage, pull yourself together." This was Sir James—all compassion, obviously.

"Aaaahhhh...Wilfred! Wilfred!" Mrs. Ramage's voice was low and cracked. I could hear Burroughs wheezing and then, as Sir James stepped aside, saw the old butler's ashen face cradled in Mrs. Ramage's arms as he fought for breath. His white hair was disordered, and he had lost his glasses; he seemed to blink sightlessly in the light. A ghastly red welt around his neck showed how close he had come to ending it all.

Mrs. Ramage, holding him like a child, was rocking back and forth in abject grief, her cap askew, her mouth wet with slobber.

"Let him go, Mrs. R," Leonard said, leaning over her, his voice a sham of sympathy. "He's been a good and faithful servant and I'm sure a good friend to you, but his time has come."

Leonard took one of her hands and tried to pry it off Burroughs's body—but Mrs. Ramage glared up at him, madness in her eyes.

"Don't touch him! You've done enough! Oh, Wilfred, Wilfred. Why are you leaving me? Why? Why?"

"Come on, Mrs. R," Leonard said, his voice soft, coaxing. "Let me take care of him. This will make him better."

I saw with a shock what he was holding in his hand—a huge hypodermic syringe, filled with a clear liquid. Mrs. Ramage screamed—it was an unearthly noise.

"Get away! Get away from him!" I didn't have much hope for Leonard's chances against this mad creature—but there were four of them, and only one of her.

"Come on, dear," Lady Caroline said. "You've got to let

us look after him now. Everything's going to be all right." I saw her signaling to Leonard to attack Mrs. Ramage from the other side.

"You'll never take him from me."

"Why, you've worked yourself into a terrible state... Come on, just let Leonard..."

Mrs. Ramage threw her bulk across the prone form of Burroughs, nearly finishing off what he had unsuccessfully started with the rope, and shielded him from Leonard and his lethal needle.

"You mustn't! You can't! He's...he's...my brother!"

Mrs. Ramage started weeping hysterically; I could see Burroughs's white face sticking out from underneath her massive bosom. The rest of the family stood inert; even Leonard was shocked enough to lower the syringe.

"Your brother!" thundered Sir James. "Why were we not told?"

"There are things that even you don't know, Sir James," Mrs. Ramage said, fixing him with a bloodshot eye. "Life belowstairs at Drekeham Hall is more complicated than you imagine."

Just as I opened my ears for the confession that would make sense of the insane jumble of the last forty-eight hours, I felt a light touch on my ankle. Repressing a gasp, I turned—and, in the gloom, saw the thing I wanted to see more than anything else in the world. Morgan's face.

He had crawled noiselessly along the passage—obviously, he was shaping up to be a very useful detective's sidekick indeed—and he was holding Sergeant Kennington's gun. In my hurry to leave the room, I had completely forgotten about it.

Of course, we could not talk, but this didn't stop Morgan from expressing his delight and relief at finding me alive and well. He clambered on top of me—there was just about room for this in the cramped tunnel—and started kissing me on the mouth, face, and neck. I struggled to pay attention to what was going on beyond the door.

"There's been quite enough trouble from belowstairs," Lady Caroline said. "It's time to put a stop to all this nonsense. Mrs. Ramage: let him go."

"Never!" Mrs. Ramage screamed.

Morgan had his hands down my trousers and was fingering my ass; he hadn't yet fucked me, and I got the sense that this was the one and only thing on his mind.

"Leonard, for God's sake," Lady Diana said, her voice cruel and commanding, "put the old bastard out of his misery. You'd do the same for any dog."

Mrs. Ramage wailed, and there was a terrible crunching noise.

"Aaaaagh!" Lady Diana screamed. "The old bitch is biting me! Get her off!"

Through the crack I could see an undignified scramble, on the outskirts of which danced Leonard, his syringe glinting in the light as he tried to find an unhindered shot at Burroughs.

Morgan, who had been chewing on my ear while he worked his fingers up my ass, suddenly stopped dead. He had found what Sergeant Kennington had missed, and pulled it out. He was so astonished at finding an inanimate object embedded in my ass that he remained totally dumbfounded.

Pulling his hand out of my trousers, I grabbed the gun from him and burst through the low door into Leonard's room, just in the nick of time; he had Burroughs's shanks in his sights and was about to administer the lethal shot.

"Stop right there!" I shouted. "I've got a gun!"

Lady Caroline screamed, Leonard froze, and Mrs. Ramage released Diana's leg from her yellowing teeth.

"Mitchell! Put that down! What do you think you're doing!" Sir James said.

"I'm trying to stop you from committing another murder."

"Another murder? How dare you!"

But I had hit the mark; all the defiance went out of him. I pointed the gun at Leonard. "Drop the syringe."

"You'll never fire. You wouldn't dare..."

I squeezed the trigger and shot a few inches above his shoulder. The bullet hit one of his Chinese vases, which exploded with satisfyingly dramatic effect.

"I said, drop the syringe."

Leonard obeyed this time, and I stamped the horrible thing into the floor.

"Oh, I say... My rug..."

Morgan had by now emerged into the room as well, and made himself useful by kneeing Leonard in the groin—something I suspect he'd been longing to do for some time—and then disengaging the half-suffocated Burroughs from Mrs. Ramage's embrace. The fight went out of her, and she slumped back on the couch like an overstuffed rag doll.

Burroughs was in a bad way. The rope had damaged his windpipe, and his recent crushing had robbed him of air. It was clear that he was struggling for life. Morgan laid him gently on the floor and placed a cushion under his head. In the ensuing silence, all we could hear was Burroughs's labored breath, and the occasional groan from a doubled-up Leonard.

Just as it seemed that the old man was about to expire in front of our very eyes, one white, clawlike hand scrabbled toward my feet and clutched at my trousers. I crouched beside him.

"What is it, Burroughs?"

"Meeks..."

"I know. Don't worry. We'll get him."

"Meeks... Rex..."

Lady Caroline screamed, and I thought for a moment she was going to throw herself on the poor old butler and rip his throat out. I quelled her impulse with a wave of the gun.

"What about Rex, Burroughs? Meeks and Rex?"

"Yes." He sighed with relief.

"You mean..."

Burroughs struggled to speak, and his voice was halting and hoarse. "As soon as Charlie laid his eyes on him, he knew. Rex felt the same. I tried to warn them..."

"You filthy old man," Diana said, the muscles in her jaw working. "You disgusting pimp. How dare you speak of Rex in that way?"

Burroughs was past caring; he knew he was dying. He laughed weakly at Diana's fury. "Oh, that was true love. The truest love I've ever seen. They didn't care about upstairs and downstairs."

"Why couldn't he just fuck him and be content with that," Leonard said, having recovered enough to speak. "Everyone else in this wretched house does that, don't they, James? Up and down the back passage, up and down, all the footmen and the gardeners and the stable lads and the hall boys. We've had them all, haven't we? And then Rex has to go and fall in love, the dirty swine."

"I will not believe it," Lady Caroline bellowed. "No son of mine..."

"Be quiet, Caroline," Sir James said. "It's over."

Burroughs was struggling for breath. "That's where Charlie was on the afternoon of the poor gentleman's murder. In his room with Rex. Together, like they always were whenever they could be."

"That is a lie!" Diana hissed. "Rex was with me."

"And Meeks was serving tea in here, I believe," Leonard said.

"Oh, no," Burroughs said, laughing weakly. "I'm afraid not. And there's proof. I took photographs."

"Wilfred!" Mrs. Ramage said, having recovered from her hysteria. "Don't tell them!"

"Yes, it's true," Burroughs said, barely able to whisper now. "I didn't just watch them, Mr. Mitchell, all the young men in Drekeham Hall. I took pictures as well. At first it was just for my own amusement, but then we started to sell them. All that footman's idea, that terrible young man I told you about. He had the contacts in London. Got me to supply them. Posed for the pictures. Even entertained some of the clients here. We had quite a little business going. He introduced a few of his friends. That's where young Hibbert came from. And there were others—some down here, some in London. Poor Mr. Walworth..."

Sir James gasped and cursed; then there was silence.

"I'm sorry, Sir James," Burroughs said. "I cannot let Charlie go to the hangman. It's not right."

"None of it's right," Sir James said, gloomily. Lady Caroline, however, was less easily persuaded.

"You'll never make the police believe that all of this was going on in Drekeham Hall, Mr. Burroughs. You underestimate the respect with which the police treat their betters."

"Especially when they're so handsomely paid by them," I said. "I know all about your deal with Sergeant Kennington."

"You know nothing," she spat. "And nobody will believe you. Go ahead, tell the world whatever you want. See how far you get."

"But the photographs..." Burroughs whispered. "The photographs..."

"They have been destroyed, along with everything else in your disgusting darkroom. How dare you use my property for such vileness?"

"Oh, dear..." Burroughs was ebbing fast. "Charlie... I'm so sorry..."

"You see, your nasty little scheme has backfired," Lady Diana said.

"I wouldn't be so sure," I said. "Morgan?"

"Mitch?"

"Would you be so kind as to hand me...that object that you found?"

He rummaged in his pocket and rather gingerly produced the canister of film. It wasn't in the best of condition, and I hoped to God that my ass juices hadn't damaged the contents.

"Is this what you were looking for?"

Lady Diana made a grab for the film, but Morgan stepped in front of me.

"You don't want to touch that, Whopper," he said. "You don't know where it's been."

I held all the cards, not to mention one slightly fetid roll of film, in my hands. And I had a gun. It seemed we'd won.

And then, with a horrible rattle, Burroughs breathed his last. His head twitched convulsively to one side, and he was dead.

Total silence reigned in the room, save for the ticking of one of Leonard's hideous ormolu clocks.

And then came a weird gurgling that became a rumble that became a groan, then a scream; Mrs. Ramage, insane at last, threw herself on the body of her brother.

"Wilfred!" she screamed over and over again. "Wilfred! My Wilfred"!

Sir James leaned down to try to comfort her, which was brave.

"My dear Mrs. Ramage," he said. "Your grief does you credit. But this is excessive, even in a sister."

Mrs. Ramage looked up, suddenly silent, and then let forth the most unearthly laugh I have ever heard.

"Sister? Sister! I'm not his sister!"

"But you said..."

"No! I am Wilfred's brother!"

And then, with one final, ghastly shriek, she ran from the room.

All was chaos. Lady Diana collided with the fleeing housekeeper and landed with a thud against Leonard's inlaid sideboard, sending bibelots showering in all directions. Leonard attempted to slip out the back passage but was sent sprawling by another well-aimed blow from Morgan's foot. In the confusion, Sir James jumped on me, wrested the gun from my grip, and started waving it about his head.

"Stop, all of you! Stop!"

His voice commanded instant obedience.

We watched with horror as he turned the gun on himself, and placed it against the roof of his mouth.

I saw his finger tensing on the trigger.

Everything happened at once. A figure in blue threw himself through the door, rugby-tackled Sir James to the floor, and disarmed him. Not Sergeant Kennington, as I first suspected, but PC Shipton. I knew he would come in handy.

Leonard took advantage of the melee to dart for the door, and slipped out—only to be brought back in, seconds later, kicking and screaming, in the iron grip of a tall, broad-shouldered young blond man.

"Rex, old chap!" Morgan said. "Where the hell have you been?"

"Hello, Boy," Rex said, cool as a cucumber. "Sit down, Uncle Leonard." He forced Leonard into a chair. "I say— where's Mama?"

I looked around. Lady Caroline had gone.

XIII

THE REST OF OUR STORY BELONGS, REALLY, TO REX EAGLE, as it was to him that we looked for explanations. These came after dinner that night—a more informal affair than most dinners at Drekeham Hall, given the state of chaos belowstairs. The French chef, his temperament disturbed by the events of the weekend, had a fit of the vapors and refused to cook, so Morgan and I raided the larder and prepared a cold collation. It was, if I do say so myself, delicious.

Once again at the table, but what a different party we made from the previous night. We did not bother to dress. Sir James was indisposed and shut himself up in his room. Lady Caroline had disappeared, Lady Diana had motored to London, and Leonard was in police custody, charged with the attempted murder of Wilfred Burroughs. This left Rex, his sister Belinda, Morgan, and me—plus a couple of guests in the form of Vince West, Sir James's secretary, and Charlie Meeks, bruised and cut free at last. "He's never going to leave my side again," Rex said, as he seated Meeks at the table. "I nearly lost him through my cowardice and lies. I'm not going to let that happen again. From now on, Charlie is as much part of this family as I am." There was a moment of awkwardness, but then Morgan set the tone by saying "Three cheers for Rex and Charlie!" and we drank to their health. Belinda blushed, but she kissed her brother and his friend and said that she never could stand Whopper Hunt anyway.

After we had polished off a cold chicken, half a ham, the best part of a jar of pickled onions, plus large quantities of bread and cheese—everyone had an appetite that night—Belinda went to look after her father, leaving the rest of us to hear Rex's extraordinary narrative of the last two days.

"It was Mother's idea to do away with Reg Walworth," he said, with a heavy sigh. "I can't bear to say it, but I hope that the law will catch up with her and make her pay for what she's done. Walworth was a wretch, but he did not deserve to die, and I can never forgive my mother for plotting his murder. It's true he was blackmailing Father, and trying to bust up my wedding plans—if only he'd known what a favor he was doing me!—but his crimes were nothing compared with what Mother planned. Leonard introduced her to Sergeant Kennington, a corrupt policeman he'd met at some club in London, who was prepared to do the dirty work for a vast sum of money that would guarantee his silence. I believe it was his plan to blackmail Father in his turn after the event, but that will emerge at his trial."

"Where is he now, Rex?" I asked. I'd last seen Kennington unconscious on the housekeeper's floor, covered in my spunk.

"I don't know. He's disappeared. I suspect he's with Mother. I suspect they'll try to flee the country; may already have done so. They'll be found."

"And how did Walworth die?"

"Strangled with a belt."

I rubbed my neck, remembering Kennington's predilection for asphyxia. How close had I come to losing my life?

"The murder took place in Leonard's room, just as he told you, Mitch. But the rest of it was lies. There was no sex party going on. Charlie was present for a while, but only to serve tea before the crime was committed. Poor Walworth; he thought he'd pulled off the coup of his career, and got himself accepted in a family that would set him up for the rest of his life. Little did he know that the tea and sandwiches and polite conversation were a prelude to him being lured off by Kennington and throttled. The body was dragged to a cupboard—and the rest you know."

"But why was Charlie arrested?"

Rex placed his hand over Charlie's. "They'd wanted Charlie out of the way for ages. The number of times Mother and Father tried to fire him—but either I stood in their way, or Burroughs did. In his own quiet way, Burroughs was courageous—though now we know that behind that polite facade he was exploiting the situation in the most dangerous way. Imagine the scandal if photographs of Charlie and me had started circulating in London!"

"Don't worry about that, Rex. You can keep hold of the film now."

"Finally, however, they found the perfect pretext for getting Charlie out the way for good, by blaming him for Walworth's death and counting on Kennington to block any attempt at exonerating him. It's amazing how quickly and quietly you can dispose of a human life; all you have to do is whisper the words *queer* and *murderer*, and an innocent man will go to his death. It was Leonard's idea to 'kill two birds with one stone,' as he put it: to get rid of Reg Walworth, and then to use that crime as a way of getting rid of Charlie. With both of them taken care of, there were no longer any obstacles to my marriage, and the many financial benefits dependent on it."

"But if you knew all this was going on, why didn't you try to stop it?"

"I didn't know. Oh, I had my suspicions for a long time about Father's friendship with Reg Walworth—but I had no idea he was blackmailing him. And it was only during that dreadful tea party that I learned of the murder plot. I tried to stop them, but what could I do? Kennington hinted that any interference on my part would lead to a prosecution, and disgrace, and prison, for both me and Charlie. And so I kept my mouth shut, for which I will be eternally ashamed."

He hung his head. Charlie put an arm around Rex's shoulder and kissed his blond hair.

"You can't blame yourself, Rex," Morgan said. "You did what you did for good reasons."

"And then I left them, because I couldn't stand what they were doing, and I tried to forget it all in Charlie's arms. That's where I was when Kennington killed Walworth, as you know, and as Burroughs saw. I left him to go and join in the game of Sardines, and make everything look as normal as possible—but then Belinda found the body, the police were all over the house, and before I knew it Charlie was in the back of a van being taken into the village. I tried to take the car and follow him, but Hibbert was under strict instructions to keep the garage locked. And so I ran to the village and demanded his release—but I might as well have been talking to a stone wall. The desk sergeant even denied he was there."

"Brown."

"Exactly. I tried to get past him, to find Charlie, but there was nothing I could do—and when Kennington came out to threaten me again, I ran out of ideas. And so I got the first train to London."

"That's just what I don't get, Rex," Morgan said. "Why on earth did you run away like that? Looked so damn suspicious."

"I needed bargaining power, because as long as they had Charlie, and the threat of exposing me, they held all the cards in their hands. But I knew that if I came up to London and found Walworth's lodgings, I would be able to procure proof of the very thing that they were trying, above all, to wipe out. I'd seen the blackmail notes that Walworth had sent to Father—complete with his address in Bethnal Green. I got to London by dinner time, went straight to the address, praying that Kennington's cronies hadn't got there before me. I was in luck; the landlady knew nothing of her tenant's disappearance, and was obviously used to 'posh gents,' as she put it, turning up at all hours of the day and night. For a small consideration of a five-pound note, she gave me a pass key to his room and said she'd 'turn a blind eye.'

"Walworth's lodgings were grim; he hardly had a stick of furniture, and there was one very shiny suit hanging in the cupboard with a couple of shirts—all the clothes he owned, apart from the ones he died in. Oh, he must have dreamed of wealth and comfort, the poor bastard. And he thought Father would pay for all that, in return for... Well, you know what. I can't blame Father. He was a handsome kid, a year younger than me, part-time stevedore, part-time boxer, but too lazy to put his mind to anything that would really give him a chance to better himself. Too addicted to easy money and easy pleasure. Bad luck that he fell in with a bad lot who showed him the way to make money out of his good looks."

"And did you find what you were looking for?"

"Oh, yes. Mr. Walworth was a very busy boy, very industrious in all the wrong areas. There were letters—not just from Father, but from half a dozen other men of wealth and influence, some of whom I know personally. I would never have guessed that the foreign secretary was... Well, anyway, I took everything I could find and I will return it all to its rightful owners. It's amazing what a man will put down in writing in the heat of passion. Reg Walworth had certainly inspired some flights of fancy—and Father was mad about him. Well, poor Dad must be suffering now."

"Don't worry, old chap," Morgan said. "Billie's looking after him."

"I think, in his way, he hoped for a real friendship with Reg. He had plans for him. He was paying for accountancy classes at a business college. But of course all the money was squandered."

"So all those payment for decorating and building work..." West said.

"Yes. Presents, patronage, whatever you want to call it. Father was always generous with his money."

"And Walworth just got greedy," I said.

"I'm afraid so," continued Rex. "That's the danger of relationships between the classes, where money is involved. Thank God nothing like that has ever come between me and Charlie."

"I don't want your money, Rex," Meeks said. He spoke rarely but to the point. "I just want you."

They looked into each other's eyes—Rex's were dark blue, surrounded by dark lashes and eyebrows that contrasted strikingly with his wavy blond hair, while Meeks's were soft and brown and deep—and I have never in my life seen a look of such true love pass between two men. I almost felt we should leave them alone.

"It was too late to come back up to town last night," Rex said, "so I stayed at the club and didn't get a wink of sleep. I was so worried about what they might do to Charlie in the police station. I can't stand the idea that they hurt you and I wasn't there to protect you, Charlie. I would have given my life..."

"There's no need for that now."

Rex took a deep breath, contained his emotion, and continued. "In the morning, I telephoned Father and told him that unless Charlie was released today, I myself would continue Walworth's work of blackmail and would send his letters to every newspaper in the country. He refused to listen, and kept telling me that it was all for the best. He had lost someone, I suppose, and wouldn't hear reason. Then I said I would break off my engagement with Diana, and tell her family the reason why I was doing it, that I loved Charlie and would rather live with him in honest poverty than carry on living a luxurious lie. That stung him, I think, and he slammed the receiver down. Every time I rang after that I was told that Sir James was out."

"Sorry about that, Mr. Eagle," West said. "I was instructed not to put through any calls."

"I don't blame you, West. I'm glad I didn't speak with him, because I would have said terrible things. Instead I went to my solicitor's house in Kensington—and he wasn't too delighted to see me on a Sunday morning, but the Eagle account is worth a bit of inconvenience, or used to be—and deposited all the papers with him, instructing him that he was to send them out to certain editors if he didn't hear from me by tomorrow morning. Don't worry—I called him before dinner and told him all was well. The letters will be returned to the men who wrote them.

"He also advised me to go straight to Scotland Yard with my allegations about Kennington's part in the affair, and thus effect his removal from Drekeham. When they catch up with him, Kennington is in for a very nasty time of it indeed.

"That done, I caught the train back down to Drekeham as fast as I could—but you know how slow the Sunday service can be, and it was teatime before I arrived. I went straight to the police station—and again I was refused entry, or access to Charlie. But this time, as I was leaving, I met a young policeman—"

"Shipton."

"Yes. You know him, Mitch?"

"I do." I think I must have blushed.

"Well, thank God, he turned out to be an honest copper, and he told me that he didn't like what was going on in the police station and that, if we were quick about it, we'd be able to overpower Brown while Kennington was out of the way. Kennington was back here, of course—and he'd been sent to deal with you, Mitch, and Morgan. Shipton seemed very distressed about this. You must have made a big impression on him."

"Oh, he's just crazy about Americans."

Morgan looked sidelong at me and groped me under the table.

"Shipton pretended that we were having a fight, Brown came outside to sort me out, and we turned on him. He was easy to overpower, and we left him locked up in the cell. The rest of the station was unguarded; it was Piggott's day off, can you believe. So we found Charlie, and I was so glad to see him alive that I didn't realize how badly he'd been hurt."

"I'm all right," Meeks said, his face still badly marked. "Though I must say that some of your kisses were a bit painful."

I thought it best not to mention the treatment I had seen him getting from Piggott and Kennington, who had presumably been abusing him all weekend. Little wonder Piggott needed his day off. And he'd need all his energies for "interrogating" Leonard on Monday. I imagined that Leonard would approve of his methods.

"Well, I like a happy ending," I said, with a pang of jealousy. Rex and Charlie were so sure of each other; I was less certain of Morgan, who, despite being crazed with lust, was still speaking with great enthusiasm of his forthcoming marriage to Belinda.

"We'd never have done it without you, Mitch, and you, Morgan," Rex said. "If you hadn't uncovered Leonard and

Mrs. Ramage...I shudder to think what might have happened."

"Speaking of Mrs. Ramage," I said, "whatever happened to her—or should I say him?"

"I saw her running out of the house and across the lawn from my room, where Sir James had sent me," West said. "He'd told me to stay there and not come out until I was called for. But there was so much noise and confusion in the house that when I saw Mrs. R screaming like a lunatic and heading for the cliffs, I thought I'd better follow. Fortunately, she's a large lady, and she can't run very fast, whereas I used to be rather good at track events at Cambridge..."

"Go on, Vince."

"Well, I caught up with her on the other side of the rhododendrons and tried to stop her—but she punched me in the stomach and winded me. She may have looked like a woman, but she punched like a man. By the time I'd picked myself up she had reached the edge of the cliff and was calling her brother's name. Her hair had come down from its bun, and there was a huge bald patch on top of her head. She started ripping off her clothes, and of course most of it was padding. I wonder how long she's lived like that?"

"We may never know."

"I managed to pull her to the ground before she could do herself any more mischief, and then I did something I'm rather ashamed of. I hit a woman."

"She's not a woman, Vince," I said.

"Well, in any case, I punched her lights out and then carried her all the way back to the house in a fireman's lift."

"My God," I said, looking at West in a new light, "you're stronger than you look."

"Well, I had to take quite a few breaks," he said, modestly. "I put her in the kitchen and called the doctor. They've taken her away to hospital. I think she's gone completely mad."

"I hope they look after her," Rex said. "She may have been strange, but she was a jolly good housekeeper."

"What I don't understand," Morgan said, "is why she was so desperate to protect Sir James. Why would she involve herself in a murder that had nothing to do with her? She was only an employee."

"That's the saddest thing of all," Rex said. "It was loyalty of a kind. Loyalty is a good, fine thing, but when it goes bad, and turns to blindness, it's a terrible danger. Mrs. Ramage worshipped Father and Mother—and now that we know her secret, perhaps we can understand why. Here, in Drekeham Hall, she was safe, and she was a woman. Anything that threatened to turn her out..."

"I see," Morgan said. "Dashed funny family I'm marrying into."

Eventually we drifted off to our own rooms for our final night at Drekeham Hall—but not before one final revelation.

I planned to return to Cambridge the following day, while Morgan was taking Belinda and Sir James to London, ostensibly to look for Lady Caroline, but more, Morgan said, "to have a bit of a jolly after all this misery."

"I'll get Hibbert to drop you all at the station in the morning," Rex said. "Unless you'd like to take the car, Boy?"

"Oh, that would be fun," Morgan said, "if Hibbert doesn't mind."

"I'll ask him," Rex said. "By the way, has anyone seen him this evening?"

Nobody had.

A quick search of the servants' quarters revealed that he, too, had flown the coop—much to the chagrin of Susie, the kitchen maid, to whose savings he had helped himself before leaving.

"Where on earth has he got to?" Rex said, furious.

"I imagine he's with Lady Diana," I said, nervously.

"Why on earth... Oh. You mean they were..."

"I'm afraid so, Rex."

"Well, rather him than me. I've got what I want. Good night." And with that he took Charlie Meeks to his room and, for the first time, they were together without fear or concealment.

My night was less happy.

As soon as we were in our bedroom, Morgan pounced on me and started ripping my clothes off, but I pushed him gently away.

"What's the matter, Mitch? Gone off me?"

"Of course I haven't. It's just that, after tomorrow, things are never going to be the same again."

"'Course they are. Think of all the fun we'll have in Cambridge next term."

"You'll be getting married, and before you know it you'll be leaving college and starting work, and I won't have you any more."

"Come on, you chump. Don't be gloomy. I told you from the start that I was crazy about Belinda, and I still am. We're going to have a proper family, not like this lot. But that doesn't mean that you won't be my best pal."

"But I want more than that."

"I can't give you more than that, Mitch." He took my hands and placed them on his ass. "You can have this any time you want it. And this..." He put his mouth over mine, and kissed it. "And this..." He stepped back and pulled his hard cock out of his fly, waving it at me.

"But what about this?" I laid a hand over his heart, which was beating hard through his shirt, making his prick pulse.

He stepped back. "That belongs to someone else. I'm sorry, Mitch. But that's the way it is."

We stood and looked at each other.

"We were a good team, Boy."
"We'll always be that."
"Will we?"
"I hope so."
"But you don't love me as you love Belinda."
"No. Sorry."

He was honest, and had always been honest. And as I gazed sadly at him as if for the last time, he pulled his shirt over his head, kicked off his shoes and socks, and removed his pants. He stood naked before me—the beautiful, slim, dark Harry Morgan, with his messy black hair, his trusting handsome face, and his cock as stiff as an iron bar, just as it always was.

Did I love him? I'd convinced myself that I did. I wanted him, certainly—and my plan to seduce him had been far more successful than I had ever dreamed. More successful, to tell the truth, than my attempts at sleuthing, which were, at best, hit or miss.

But love? Love as Rex and Charlie knew it? Love even as Sir James had felt for Reg Walworth—an infatuation, an *amour fou* that would lead a man to risk everything? No—I didn't feel those things for Harry Morgan. I wanted to spend time with him, to have adventures with him, to fuck him and be fucked by him. But for the rest of my life?

That reminded me of something that Morgan hadn't forgotten all day: he had not yet fucked me.

I grabbed his cock, kissed him on the mouth and set about rectifying that oversight.

EPILOGUE

Mr. and Mrs. Henry Morgan, otherwise Boy and Belinda, were married in Drekeham parish church on a beautiful day in October. Sir James gave the bride away, but remained silent and thoughtful throughout the ceremony and absented himself as soon as possible from the wedding breakfast. Lady Caroline was unable to attend, being detained in a Belgian prison whence she was about to be extradited to England to face charges of conspiracy to murder. Rex attended with Charlie Meeks, both of them as handsome as matinee idols in their morning suits, and, despite some initial tutting and whispering from the guests, they were soon the stars of the show. Morgan's family, who were Methodists, pretended that nothing out of the ordinary was going on—may, in fact, have thought nothing of it.

I was best man, and faced that rather solemn duty with as much good humor as I could muster. Of course I'd taken Morgan out the night before, we'd drunk too much, and ended up fucking each other's brains out in our room above the village pub. In the morning, he'd been so jittery (and hungover) that I'd had to suck him off, and then come in his face, before he would calm down, bathe, and dress. I knew that Morgan's powers of recovery were such that there would be plenty left for his blushing bride, come the wedding night.

Morgan did not return to Cambridge, but took a job instead in Sir James's firm, in which he proved himself an able, enthusiastic worker, and he soon rose through the ranks, filling a vacuum left by Sir James's own withdrawal from public life and Rex's decision that he could no longer work for his father. Within a year, the company was back on its feet, the coffers were full—and Morgan and Belinda were the proud parents of a beautiful daughter. They live in London, I see them frequently, and Morgan and I remain as close as ever. I am happy to say that my romantic longings in that direction have changed into a lasting affection, a friendship spiced by occasional, athletic bouts of sex.

Sir James spent the months after the death of Reg Walworth in a black depression, barely talking to his children. The scandal took a terrible toll on him—and even though Barrett's report in the papers the week after the murder had presented a highly sanitized version of events, there was enough suggestion of wrongdoing in the death of the "unemployed young man" who was "in Sir James's intimate circle" and in "Lady Caroline's desertion with her chauffeur" to ensure that Sir James, once a man of power and influence, was obliged to retire. Drekeham Hall was like a haunted house; without Burroughs or Mrs. Ramage, who recovered slowly in a private clinic, at Sir James's expense, the household rapidly fell to pieces. Wages were unpaid, and the chef left, followed by the kitchen maid and the rest of the indoor staff, with the exception of Simon, the deaf-mute hall boy, who was left to attend to Sir James's every need. The gardener and the stable boy remained, happy to tend the grounds and the horses—and each other, I was sure.

It was Simon who eventually coaxed Sir James out of his private hell and back to life. I never knew exactly how it happened, but little by little he became not just a servant but a friend, a mainstay—and, of course, a lover. Sir James found in Simon, with his docile nature, his smooth skin, and his quiet endurance of a hard life, exactly the companion he needed. Simon and Sir James now live quietly together in a few rooms of the huge house that so recently had been turned over to chaos.

Leonard Eagle did not exactly turn over a new leaf, but he was sufficiently chastened by his experiences to keep well away from the rest of the family, and settled into a life in London that made it unlikely their paths would ever cross again. The charge of attempted murder was dropped on the ground of insufficient evidence; I imagine that Sir James was behind that. After two days of incarceration in Drekeham Police Station, Leonard was a free man, and he was never seen in the village again. Funnily enough, neither was PC Piggott. I suspect, but do not know for certain, that this was no coincidence. Sergeant Kennington reappeared, as Rex had predicted, to attempt blackmail of Sir James; he was rapidly apprehended, tried, and hanged. Much as I deplore the death penalty, I couldn't help thinking that this was a suitable end for a man who had shown such a flair for strangling.

PC Shipton was promoted, and now runs the station, where I visit him occasionally for a smoke.

Lady Diana Hunt made a new life for herself in Paris and soon became a regular fixture in the gossip columns on both sides of the English channel, notorious for her excessive lifestyle, her fashionable cocaine use, and her string of engagements to men from all walks of life, most of them rough working types. Of Hibbert we never heard again. I am sure that someone, male or female, is willing to pay handsomely for his considerable charms.

And me? I returned to Cambridge and continued with my postgraduate studies. It was a lonely place without Morgan, but I had much to do, and I was soon enjoying my new role as a tutor to a new generation of undergraduates, who learned much under my guidance. After the excitements of the summer, however, I found myself longing for new cases to crack—but that's another story.

And to my delight and surprise, I found myself with a new roommate—none other than Vincent West, Sir James's former secretary, who left Drekeham Hall and was allowed to resume his Cambridge studies after the college authorities were persuaded that he had been unjustly sent down. The moment he arrived in Cambridge, he looked me up and proposed a beer at a small pub by the river.

He appeared younger than when I had last seen him at Drekeham Hall; liberated from his lonely life and the burden of responsibility, he had flowered. He stood straight, his eyes shone, his skin was no longer pale and pasty but tanned by the sun. And no sooner had we sat down with our pints in the garden, savoring a day of early-autumn sunshine under the golden leaves of a chestnut tree, than he delivered a carefully prepared speech.

"Mitch, I hope you won't think I'm being forward, but ever since I first saw you at Drekeham Hall, I've thought of nothing else all summer. I nearly wrote to you a thousand times, but I never posted the letter, because I thought that you and Morgan...well, you know. But now he's married, and you're here on your own, and I'm here on my own...well..."

His words faltered.

"I had it all worked out, but now it makes no sense."

"Just say it, Vince."

"Damn it, Mitch, I just want you so badly it hurts."

That was all that needed to be said.

"Finish your beer, Vince," I said, and downed mine in

one gulp. "We're going back to my rooms. And you're staying."

How we made it up the staircase I don't know; we were already tearing at each other's clothes the minute we entered the building. The door slammed behind us, and we devoured each other with kisses. We didn't make it as far as my narrow single bed; instead, we made love on the threadbare rug in front of the empty fireplace, the last rays of the sun shining through the window and onto our naked flesh. He was passionate—perhaps the most passionate lover I have ever known, with months, years, of frustration pent up inside him. When I entered him, as he lay on his back, his legs resting on my shoulders, I thought he was going to cry with joy.

We didn't leave the room until hunger drove us to the refectory. He moved right in the next day, and the college very grudgingly gave us another narrow bed. Pushed together, these were ample for our needs.

And so we lived, worked, and loved together for the rest of the year. My thesis is nearly finished; Vince will graduate with flying colors. When I return to Boston in the fall, he will be by my side.

THE END